The Serial Club

B.D. Carlson

Edited by C.K. Carlson

Published with the assistance of Apathy Productions LLC

https://apathyproductions.com/

Table of Contents

Chapter 1

The air was dead still silent as the Old Springs Community Police Department, dressed up in militarized body armor and armed with laser-sighted AR-15s, surrounded the rundown, grass- and dirt-stained ranch house, poised for entry. On the signal, they breached the front door with a battering ram and threw flashbangs into the home, causing blinding light and a series of deafening explosions.

Once all was settled, the dozen-plus cops swarmed the now pitch-black home, equipped with night vision goggles, guns drawn, ready to engage. They had been instructed to shoot on sight due to the potential for escalation. Officers were hoping that any remaining hostages were no longer alive and would not pose an issue for the shoot-on-sight directive. If there were complications, the captain had said to make the best call possible, and everyone would be backed up from above during any inquest.

Inside the decrepit ranch home, there was little more than the accumulated filth of years of living amid abusive behavior. No apparent signs of struggle, trauma, or overt criminal activity were to be seen. As the squads proceeded through the home and approached the back hallway, an agent from the task force noticed that a heavily worn area rug was somewhat askew. He pushed the rug aside with his foot and saw the outline of a trapdoor. He silently signaled to his team about the discovery with a hand gesture.

After receiving silent approval to proceed, the officer bent down, grabbed the handle, and slowly pulled up the door. It was then that a horrific whiff of rotten meat and sewage came up from below, making all the cops surrounding it wince. The ladder led down to a silken blackness thick with decay, and the cops descended, one by one, into the waiting dark…

Just then, the immaculate fantasy world around him dropped away like it was never there, and in its place was a deep-throated howling boom from somewhere in the distance below.

"HUDSON!"

Oh man, how long has he been yelling for me? Hudson thought. "One sec, Dad, I'm watching '48 and 1/2 Hours.' It's my favorite show!"

"HUDSON, GET DOWN HERE, NOW!"

"10 MINUTES! It's almost over."

"Pause it NOW and get down here! I'm NOT KIDDING!"

Hudson pressed the pause button on his phone. It's un-freaking real, he thought; every single time he sat down and was enjoying himself, his father was there to make sure he unsettled Hudson immediately. It's like his dad had some sort of radar to determine whether Hudson was happy and at peace, so he needed to disrupt him.

Hudson came downstairs, hurrying but not too much. His father looked at him with the unending exasperation of a parent who doesn't understand their child or how to modify his behavior.

"Hudson, why are you watching that type of show? What kind of fourteen-year-old watches reality TV about people being MURDERED like that?"

Hudson replied in a lowered voice, his head down a bit. "It was the show Mom and I used to watch together. I guess it makes me feel like she's still around."

His father realized his callousness and lowered his voice. He changed his tone and lightly patted his son, albeit uncomfortably, on the back. "I'm sorry, son. I guess it's ok if it helps. Just not too much, all right? I don't want that stuff warping your mind."

"Yeah," Hudson replied. "It's not like video games, movies, and the news don't warp kids' minds or anything."

"Don't be a wise-ass, Hudson. Where is your brother? BRODY! GET DOWN HERE!"

The thundering sounds of a 6-foot-2-inch, 200-pound overgrown teenager thumped down the stairs, rattling the surrounding pictures and the house as he barely hit each step on his way down.

"Yeah, what's up, Dad?"

"Now, I called you two down for a reason. Hudson, it turns out Mrs. Franklin won't be able to come over and watch you after school anymore."

"Oh, that's a shame," Hudson mumbled.

"Stop it, Hudson. Now, you know I have work until at least early evening, and you can't sit alone for hours without supervision."

"Oh, I don't care, Dad. I just want to play my games, work on the computer, and watch some shows."

"Yeah, Dad," Brody said. "It's not like he has any friends you need to keep an eye on."

"Up yours, Brody!" Hudson was fuming.

"Stop it, you two. It turns out a few parents in the neighborhood have the same issue, and we have come up with a solution. Brody, we want to pay you to watch Hudson and a few other neighborhood kids after school every day until we get home from work. We will pay you $10 an hour."

"Are you kidding me, Dad? You don't think I have anything better to do? And $10? You can't be serious?"

"OK, fine, what would it take to make it worthwhile?" His father looked at him sternly. "Come on, Brody, it's not forever. Just until our schedules are a little more manageable."

"I'll do it for $20 an hour. That's like 3 hours per day. Not bad bread."

"Fine. It's done."

"Wait one sec!" Hudson inserted. "Just who is coming here that I must hang out with?"

Hudson's father put on a forced smile. "It's going to be great, Hudson. There are a few neighborhood kids whose parents work late, too. This will be good for you to have some people around."

Hudson crossed his arms. "Yeah, right. Some annoying idiots who will interrupt me and ask me stupid questions endlessly. I can't wait."

"That's enough, Hudson. Try to give it a chance, okay? In fact, you get to meet one of them right now."

Just then, there was a knock on the door, and Hudson nearly jumped out of his shoes. How much he hated loud noises and surprises. Hudson's Dad opened the door, and the most beautiful girl Hudson had ever seen stood there. All his annoyance and trepidation melted instantly, and all that was left was a warm curiosity and genuine interest.

Chapter 2

Hudson didn't interact with people in a typical fashion. It was more of a one-way data dump of all he was thinking about and all his interests, all at once. He assumed that if he found some innocuous information incredibly interesting, so must everyone else. So, he talked endlessly about his video games, favorite shows and books, and all the little things about the world, its patterns and trends, that he found fascinating. Hudson must have been talking for at least ten minutes before he realized he had never asked the new girl her name. When he focused on her, really focused on her, probably for the first time since he had seen her, she was looking at him incredulously. He also, for the first time, noticed she was African American.

"Oh, I never asked your name," Hudson said.

She looked at him for a moment, not annoyed, more curious and amused, "I'm glad you were able to catch your breath. I'm Cai."

"Huh. That's a different name. Is it short for something?"

"Yeah, it's short for my real name." She paused for a second. "I don't like my real name."

"What's your real name?"

Cai looked him up and down. "Um, we'll see." She then got a wry smile. "What do you have to do around here?"

"Well, it's just my dad and me, so not much of a house. We're lucky, though; at least, he tells me we are. Cause of his job, we get to live among all these rich people." Hudson motioned out the window to the plethora of treeless McMansions lined up evenly down the block.

"Yeah, my mom tells me the same thing. All I know is the rich kids in this school are fucking assholes."

Hudson's eyes almost popped out of his head. It's not like he didn't hear people swearing on TV and in video games and all, but to hear such a young girl say it so loudly and with such conviction, he was bowled over. As a knee-jerk reaction, he leaned in and started whispering when he replied.

"I know. I can't stand them either," he said, looking both ways to ensure no one heard. "How long since you moved here?"

"Just a few months ago. My mom works for the same company as your dad for her day job, so we get to hang out after school. Lucky us."

Hudson winced a bit. He didn't think it was noticeable, but it was very evident to Cai.

"Look," Cai said. "I don't wanna be here either. But we don't have a choice, so we might as well get along."

"Oh no, it's cool. I mean, you seem cool. I'm just not used to having people over. That's all."

Cai noticed he meant it, and she relaxed a bit. "So, you have anything to eat here?"

"Yeah, how about some cereal?"

"Great."

Hudson showed Cai to the kitchen. As he went through the list of less-than-healthy ultra-processed cereal brands, he put aside his bowl and favorite spoon so this new person wouldn't take them. Then, there was a knock at the door, and the jolt almost sent Hudson out of his shoes with shock.

"Jeez," said Cai, alarmed by his jumpiness. "It's just someone at the door. You think it's the cops?" She smiled, nodding to the door sarcastically.

"Oh no," Hudson said slowly, feeling embarrassed. "I just react strongly to loud sounds. They freak me out."

Cai looked at him curiously but didn't say anything more.

Chapter 3

Just like a few minutes earlier, a similar scene unfolded at the front door. His father answered as Hudson hung towards the back to analyze what was transpiring and exactly who was about to be inserted into his peaceful little world. It turns out it was another girl.

"HUDSON!"

"Dad, I'm right behind you."

"Oh." He lowered his voice quickly. "Hudson, this is Sage and her mother…I'm so sorry; what was your name again?"

A stout-looking, middle-aged woman with jet-black hair replied with a warm smile, "My name is Alona. Nice meeting you, Hudson." She gestured to the young lady. "This is my daughter, Sage. Is it OK if she spends some time at your house?"

Hudson immediately liked the mother. He sensed a strength and authenticity that drew him in immediately. The fact that she asked him if it was all right for someone else to come into his home meant everything to him. No one ever considered his feelings as an independent person.

"Hi, Hudson. It's nice meeting you," Sage said, smiling. She was a lovely young lady who wore all sorts of hippie-like accouterments, from feathers in her hair to beads and other types of native-looking jewelry. She seemed nice, but Hudson was sure not to trust anyone too soon. He liked her mom, but he would have to look into this Sage person.

After a brief time, Hudson led Sage into the kitchen and introduced her to Cai. The two girls acknowledged each other with some hesitation, unsure about meeting a total stranger.

"Sage, we were just about to have some cereal. Would you like to join us?" Hudson said sheepishly.

"Sure, I'd love to," Sage replied. She reached into her purse and pulled out a Ziplock baggie filled with what looked like nuts, granola, and other dried fruits.

Hudson and Cai's eyes popped open, and they almost said at the same time, trying not to laugh, "You bring your cereal in your purse?"

Sage wasn't embarrassed. She had been confronted about this multiple times before. "My Mom won't allow me to eat processed foods like cereal, so I have my own natural mix here that I bring everywhere."

"I am so sorry," Hudson said, feeling really sad about his new acquaintance's obviously abusive living situation. What parent would deny their kid's ability to eat a basic American food staple like cereal?

Sage just smiled and didn't let it bother her, "It's no big deal; I got used to it a long time ago. My Mom cares about me, that's all. This is her way of showing it."

Huh, thought Hudson. If his father took his cereal away, he would flip out. Like totally. But here is this little hippy girl, and she isn't bothered by it. Maybe he could learn something from her after all?

They picked out their cereal bowls and spoons and filled them with 2% low-fat milk. The three kids sat around the kitchen table and stared at everything in the room, but at each other, as they ate their cereal in total silence. Even Hudson, who was usually unaware of other people's feelings, saw this as unsustainable. They needed to do something together. But what? Video games were out; they couldn't eat while playing them anyway. Plus, there were three of them. That leaves one person out on any 2-player game or one person short of any 4-player game. Hudson didn't have many ideas about what to do with these interlopers.

"Um, do you guys want to watch TV while we eat?" Hudson asked.

They both chirped in unison, "Sure!" Hudson wondered if they were as uncomfortable as he was.

Hudson went to his room, returned with his large tablet, and put it on a stand so they could watch while eating. Immediately, the true crime show Hudson had been watching before they came over started.

"Oh, sorry guys, this is a show I like to watch. I can put something else on if it bothers you."

Without hesitation, both girls replied, "It's fine." Huh, Hudson thought, they are cooler than they look.

Chapter 4

This pattern repeated itself, first for days and then for weeks. Every day after school, Hudson, Cai, and Sage would walk to Hudson's house together, only a few blocks from the school. And, like clockwork, they would get bullied by some kids on the way home every few days. Either they were mocking Hudson for actually being with other people, as he was always alone and considered a creepy loner, or making fun of the new girls, Sage and Cai, calling them a variety of racist insults and homosexual slurs. As any kid not in the 'in' crowd will tell you, getting through the school day is an act of dire survival, even on the best days. It was nothing they were not used to.

Cai was the only one who would say anything back; she didn't seem afraid of anyone. Sometimes, they would howl back at Cai, making mocking wolf sounds. Hudson didn't understand the insult, and Cai wouldn't say anything about it when he inquired. He figured it was racial, and he should not pry too much. Hudson was amazed by her confidence and strength, though. He felt much safer with her around, although he could never really admit that to himself.

Their time together at Hudson's always started with the traditional bowl of cereal while they watched various programs. Most of them are fairly lurid and gory true crime shows. They watched all of them, sometimes multiple episodes back-to-back. Everything from Slaughter in the Midwest to 48 and 1/2 Hours, Fateline, Forensic Flies, 20/40, and Hear No Evil. Through these shows, the kids understood how investigations took place, what crimes were committed, and what motivated cops and their suspects.

Sage and Cai quickly took to true crime, enjoying the storytelling and mystery. For Hudson, it was all about getting lost in a fantasy world where he was utterly detached from reality. He didn't realize it then, but he could totally detach from his present surroundings while enjoying a TV show, movie, or book. He noticed most other people would do these things in the background or as a side activity. But not for Hudson. He got fully into whatever he was doing at the time, one hundred percent. Well, if he liked what he was doing. Otherwise, he just disconnected, silent, and maudlin to the point that it worried people about what may be wrong with him.

But with Cai and Sage, and maybe for the first time, Hudson felt like two people really understood him and didn't judge him for whatever idiosyncrasies he may have had. While Hudson has his quirks, he is gentle as could be and would never think about hurting any other being, human or otherwise. Both Cai and Sage instinctively knew how solid Hudson was as a person. They were also aware there was something different about him. He was cool and detached, but if you engaged him, he was brilliant and had much to say. Hudson couldn't leap to actually engage other people willingly, though. They had to come to him.

After the traditional cereal-and-murder show (their name for true crime programs), the three usually played video games on their tablets. Always present, but never too near, was the somewhat comforting specter of Hudson's big brother, Brody, who would usually be on the phone in his room or the backyard playing with his new drone. He didn't interact with the kids too much; he just yelled something obnoxious from another room at Hudson once in a while. He was kept in check by the presence of two girls, which prevented him from being too obnoxious or gross. There was a definite feeling among the younger kids that, if something truly horrible were to happen, a larger adult would be there to help deal with it until their parents got home. At least, that was the idea.

Sage and Cai's parents would come to pick them up from anywhere between five and seven in the evening, depending on how late they had to work. Then Hudson would settle into his routine with his brother, Brody, and his father. This usually consisted of Hudson trying to enjoy himself alone in his room, at peace, while his father occasionally tried to engage him, unsuccessfully. Brody would occasionally try to mock and irritate him, though not very successfully.

All in the life of a fourteen-year-old boy, Hudson thought. But then he thought, what do I know, how is it for other fourteen-year-olds? Maybe they do have it worse. But, to be fair, Hudson believed he was forced to live in unreasonable conditions. The Wi-Fi was barely usable, and you couldn't move around much or risk losing a connection. His tablet was so old that other kids used to make fun of him, so now he didn't take it out of the house. It was a Wi-Fi-only tablet, anyway. Primitive.

The nice thing about Sage and Cai is that they didn't make fun of his tablet or anything else about him. After a few days, Sage brought her tablet, and they just used it. Sage's tablet had stickers of flowers and things on it. But Hudson figured it was on the back, and he didn't have to look at it while they were watching a show, so he didn't make fun of it. Hudson felt he was very mature in that way.

Chapter 5

After a few weeks of hanging out, the three acquaintances became fast friends. Sage and Cai had developed some affection for Hudson and had taken it upon themselves to keep an eye on him. While Cai's affection for him was more of a sister towards a brother, Sage thought Hudson was adorable and brilliant, and she really liked him. But Hudson had trouble interacting with others at a similar level. From his side, he was enamored of Cai and how different she was, as well as her independence and strength. There was something in Cai that Hudson very much wanted. A sense of self and independence that he feared he would never achieve. He had more trouble understanding Sage as a person. She was so nice, empathetic, and compassionate. It's not that Hudson didn't want those things; he did, but he saw those qualities in his mother and, not surprisingly, Sage's mother, too.

These undercurrents rumble in complete silence and only occur in each individual's mind, usually without them being fully conscious of it. Into this unique situation, their world was turned upside down one afternoon when a most unexpected gift arrived on Hudson's doorstep.

During their daily walk home from school to Hudson's house, a neighborhood cat frequently accompanied them. He only allowed Hudson to pet him, and then he would scamper away, weaving in and out of the hedges as they meandered home. Both Sage and Cai commented on how much animals seemed to like Hudson. He told them he was sure animals liked him more than people did. They jokingly started calling him "The Beastmaster." Hudson liked this name very much. He understood animals, and they understood him. People, not so much.

It was on a Friday, just after school, as Hudson, Sage, and Cai were enjoying their daily bowl of cereal and watching a deep-dive documentary on famous serial killers, when Hudson heard a cat meowing at the front door through an open window. At first, they all ignored it, but the cat kept going, as if it wanted someone in the house to pay attention. Finally, Hudson opened the door, and the neighborhood cat who accompanied them on their walks was sitting on their front step. Hudson couldn't believe it.

"Holy shit, guys, our cat is here," Hudson said, genuinely surprised.

Both the girls came to the door, seeing their feline friend licking its paws on the front mat with a look of grim satisfaction on its face. All the kids briefly wondered what the cat was doing there until they looked down and saw a spit-covered lump that looked like a mouse.

"Oh," Sage said. "She brought us a present; how nice."

But it quickly dawned on each of them that it was not a mouse they were looking at. As their vision focused, their minds clicked to understand what they saw, something none had ever seen IRL before: a severed human finger.

Chapter 6

Each kid assumed they would be horrified by what they saw, but they just found it…interesting. Perhaps they were being desensitized to gore and violence while watching their murder shows daily for the past few months. Maybe it was the fact that they were all bored out of their skulls, and this 'present' represented an adventure they could go on together. Some mystery in a world that seemed incredibly unmysterious, at least to anyone with a bit of common sense who reads a book now and then. And Hudson was probably as well-read as most adults were. Actually, if we're being real, he was much more well-read than most adults.

A brief discussion began under the neighborhood cat's watchful eye, who was admiring her generous gift to her walking friends.

"Is that what it looks like?" Sage asked, bending over slightly.

"It's a finger for sure," replied Cai.

"Looks like a kid's finger to me," Hudson said. Both girls nodded in agreement. The finger looked like their fingers—a young child around their age.

Hudson bent down, wiped his glasses with a microfiber cloth, and examined the finger more closely. Aside from the dirt and cat goo covering the finger, it looked clean, if not somewhat dried out. It also seemed to have been cut off. He mentioned this to Cai and Sage, who responded that it looked…cut.

"What do we do with it?" Sage inquired.

"Take it to the cops, I guess," replied Cai. "But I'm not going, that is for sure."

"BRODY!" Hudson yelled at the top of his lungs, making sure to get a response from the older teenager who was perpetually glued to his own cell phone. Soon, the thundering of steps down the stairs followed, and an irritated "WHAT?" as he made his way to the front door to see what the excitement was all about.

"What's the matter? Did the kitty bring you a dead mouse or something? Why don't you guys throw it in the woods?" As Brody talked, his eyes focused on what he thought was a mouse, and his brain started realizing the situation wasn't quite what he thought it was. You know, in his 'I know everything about everything more than you do' teenage brain.

"Holy Shit! Is that a…finger?!?" Brody was genuinely shocked and obviously grossed out. In fact, he started turning green and wobbled on his feet a bit as he steadied himself on the door frame. Sage looked genuinely concerned for him, asking him if he was ok, while Cai and Hudson looked at each other and rolled their eyes. Gimme a break, they both thought; a big man like you can't handle a little severed finger?

"What do you think we should do with it?" Hudson asked him.

"Why are you asking me?" Brody was still regaining his composure. Looking down at the ground as he spoke.

"Because you're the adult in charge, that's why." Hudson wasn't feeling much sympathy for his brother, who had given him more crap over his life than he could fully remember. Brody wasn't ruthless for an older brother, but he was an older brother, which was enough for Hudson. No mercy, thought Hudson.

Brody shot Hudson a look, not liking that he was showing him up in front of a couple of girls. "Then take it to the police station, smart guy." Then, realizing that would not fly, he followed it up with, "Fine, I'll take you there. It's not that far, and we can walk."

Everyone stood there for a second, waiting for someone to volunteer to pick up the finger and put it in something to bring to the cops. After several seconds, Cai looked around and said irritably, "Fine, Hudson, can you get me a box and some paper towels? I'll bring it." Hudson again was amazed by Cai's confidence. He quickly ran into the garage and returned with a small used Amazon cardboard shipping box and a few paper towels. Brody was silently relieved as well. He had never been so freaked out in his life, and the fact that these little girls were not was a severe blow to his growing male ego. And that little dork Hudson was getting too mouthy for his liking. He would have to put him in his place soon. After all, this house has a pecking order, and Hudson is at the bottom of that totem pole.

Chapter 7

On the way to the police station, Brody walked half a block behind the three younger kids. He did not want to be seen by anyone who mattered. That was a smart move, as on the way, a few neighborhood kids began mocking Cai from across the block. Brody kept his head down and his distance from them. He wasn't feeling good about himself because he knew he should stand up for his brother and friends. But for a sixteen-year-old, the humiliation and shame of social rejection overwhelmed any sense of brotherly protection he may have felt.

Cai had no such qualms. She had been harassed and picked on in every school, sport, and community activity she had ever attended. She knew if she didn't defend herself now, no one would help her. No adult or big person was coming to save her; Cai knew that all too well. Because they did not share the same background, Hudson and Sage would not understand this fundamental truth for years. When you come down to it, every person is on their own in this world and is ultimately responsible for their well-being, regardless of age or situation. Put your trust in people who don't have your best interests at heart, and you are asking for trouble.

Cai responded to the hoots and howls with two extended middle fingers. Hudson winced, petrified that this would trigger the bullies to come over and beat them all mercilessly until they were near hospitalization. But that did not happen. Cai flipped them off without acknowledging them, then kept walking. Cai walked away without taking the bait. Damn, Hudson thought, she was cool.

When they entered the police station, Brody suddenly played the protective big brother role. Unreal, thought Hudson, what a hypocrite. He's only there to help me when other people are looking.

The entry to the station was basically a box encased in plexiglass. At one end, a police Sergeant was sitting behind a desk. Behind the glass, of course. It was pretty quiet, as things are in police stations in upper-class residential neighborhoods. However, that didn't stop the officer from showing signs of irritation when he saw someone approaching his desk.

"Can I help you?" the officer asked Brody in an exasperated voice, not even acknowledging the younger children's presence.

Brody was immediately intimidated and regretted coming down there. Freaking annoying kids, he thought, getting me to do this. He decided to pass it on to Hudson to deal with. Let's see how he likes it. "Hi, Officer. My brother and his friends found this on our doorstep; I guess a cat dropped it off. They weren't sure what to do with it, so they brought it here."

The officer immediately turned his attention to Hudson, "Well, what have you got?"

Hudson wasn't intimidated by authority figures like Brody. In fact, he didn't see or perceive any social status structure at all. He saw everyone and everything as the same, much to the irritation and chagrin of those who saw themselves above him. He plopped the cardboard box down on the counter, loudly and unceremoniously, and just looked at the officer, waiting for him to open it. After the officer realized this little punk would not open it, he did so himself.

After he opened the box, the officer looked back up at the kids without expression and said, "Is this some joke? He noticed none of the kids were smirking. The officer looked back into the box, tilting it slightly. "Is this a fake?" He looked back up at Hudson.

"No!" replied Hudson, almost too loudly. He was insulted that the cop would mock them and assume they were just immature kids. Hudson was no fool and didn't appreciate what he considered dimwitted adults' condescension toward him.

The cop was taken aback for a second by such a young kid speaking to him like that. He looked at the kids carefully and saw they looked sincere, but did it matter? Are these kids seriously thinking a professional police officer has time to deal with their nonsense? A severed finger or not, there was probably an innocent explanation for it. And is it his job, or the police department's job, to investigate EVERY single ridiculous concern brought to them by the neighborhood children? It's not, he thought. We are here for the cases that matter and the people that matter, to be even more honest about it. Who are these kids anyway, the Sergeant wondered.

"What's your name, son?"

"Hudson. And this is my brother Brody and my friends Sage and Cai."

"What's your LAST name, kid?" he asked with irritation.

Hudson didn't see why that was relevant. "My last name?" What a jerk this cop was.

The officer stared at Hudson in dismay. Was this little snot-nose brat giving him a hard time? It was hard to tell.

"Who are your parents?"

"My Dad oversees lawn maintenance for the Old Springs Community Association."

Yeah, just what the officer figured; some lower-class urchins are wasting his time with nonsense. "And you found this at your house?"

"Yes," replied Hudson, losing his patience with this dullard. "A cat dropped it on our porch."

The officer looked at the kids for a few moments, pretending he was lost in thought, when he had already decided what to do with them the moment they walked through the door.

"Why don't you write your name, address, and number down? I'll log this in for one of our detectives to look at, and we'll get back to you if we have any questions." Before the kids could say anything or react, the copy briskly turned around and walked away, seemingly to deal with some other, more pressing issue. It was clear to the kids that this cop had no intention of assisting them in any way, regardless of what they had brought him.

Hudson had no intention of letting this official waste of space impact his ability to find more about this mystery finger. So, without much thought, he swiped the cardboard box with his finger and walked out the door. Brody and the girls were so shocked by what Hudson had done that they quietly followed him outside.

Once outside, Brody grabbed Hudson by the arm. "What are you doing? You just grabbed that and ran out? Why the hell did I bring you here anyway?"

Hudson wasn't having it. "That clown wasn't going to do anything, and I'm not leaving this here. He'll throw it in the garbage can." On that, Hudson twisted out of his brother's grip and started walking briskly back home, with Cai and Sage walking close behind. Brody walked behind them, growing increasingly irritated by Hudson's insolent behavior.

Chapter 8

Back at the house, the three kids, minus Brody, who had quickly retired to his room, sat around the kitchen table staring intently at the cardboard box.

"What do we do with it now?" Sage asked, trying not to look directly at the box, knowing what was just inside.

Cai replied, "Well, the cops don't care. And I doubt they will do anything if we bring it to our parents. They'll tell us to take it to the cops. It will be one big game of pass the hot potato."

"Yep," Hudson confirmed. "The reaction we got from Brody and that cop is what we will get from any adult. They don't care. They don't care about anything if it doesn't affect them personally." Cai nodded in agreement.

"Yeah, but from watching all those true crime shows, it seems like the cops really do care. They show them crying and everything," inserted Sage.

"They show them pretending to cry," replied Cai. "Pay close attention; you will never see real tears, just crocodile ones. All those shows, while entertaining, are just copaganda."

"What's copaganda?" Sage asked. It was a term both Sage and Hudson had never heard before.

"Copaganda is pro-cop propaganda," Cai informed them. "I learned the term on Twitter, or what used to be Twitter. It means it is biased information meant to show cops in a positive light, not who they truly are."

"Yeah, but this finger belonged to someone, a real person," said Sage, looking concerned.

Both Hudson and Cai nodded in agreement. A person was hurt, it looked like another kid, and someone needed to do something about it. If grown-ups weren't going to step up and do what was right, why shouldn't they? It's not like they didn't have the time. For hours each day, the three of them were bored silly, and any activity would be welcome. Why not a mystery that no one else wanted to solve?

"But what do we do?" Cai inquired. "Like, what steps do we take to look into it? It's not like we have a forensics department like on the murder shows."

"Well," Hudson replied, removing his glasses and cleaning them with his microcloth, "we follow the basic process we see the cops and profilers take on the shows. What do they do first after a crime has occurred? They do door-to-door interviews; I think they call it canvassing. To find out if anyone has seen anything suspicious."

"Yeah, but we're not cops, Hudson," Cai said. "How are some random kids going to get people to answer questions about a severed finger?"

"Good question, Cai. No adult will say anything about something so serious unless we give them a good reason to. So, how do we get them to talk?" Hudson was thinking.

"What about a questionnaire?" Sage said excitedly. "Like we pretend we are doing a public survey or something, and we slip in some questions to find out if someone is missing?"

Hudson and Cai looked at each other and nodded in confirmation. "That is a great idea," Hudson said, feeding off of Sage's enthusiasm. "How is this for a plan? If you and Cai assemble a questionnaire and deliver it to houses within a few miles of us, I can use my computer to search for missing children in the local area. I'll look for articles, public files, and other internet search information, and then we can meet back here and go over everything."

The plan sounded good to them. Cai and Sage stayed at the kitchen table to put together the questions while Hudson went to his room to start his digital research.

Cai led the brainstorming since she was a born leader and plowed ahead on instinct, waiting for no one. "How the hell are we going to get someone to answer such personal questions, like did a child go missing recently? People will slam the door in our faces if we ask that."

Sage didn't doubt she was right; no one wanted to be answering doors to solicitors anyway. And solicitors asking personal questions, that won't be popular at all. "Well, we tell them we are with some public health group, doing a survey, and hand them a questionnaire. Tell them we will be back later to pick it up. We try to make it official-looking."

"That's not bad," Cai was thinking. "What is the group, though? Everyone has an issue with someone else for some reason or another nowadays."

"Tell me about it," Sage replied. "Maybe we have a couple of different questionnaires targeted at different groups. Like, the older people love all that patriotic flag-waving stuff. So, we have a patriotic form for them, and then what about another one about missing children being trafficked? That will get people all hot and bothered, making them more likely to respond. That's a big issue in the media right now."

Huh, Cai thought, I had this Sage girl marked as sweet but naive. Now, she was gaining some respect for how calculating Sage could be. "I like it. We go up there all sweet and whatnot to win them over. And let's dress and act like church kids when we give them our form. How could they resist us?" Cai was smiling.

And she was right. After they got Hudson to help them with professional-looking color-printed questionnaires, they made two versions, all complete with American flags and Save the Children iconography. Then they dressed up in what was closest to their Sunday best and went house to house to 'canvas' for information on a missing child.

As expected, some houses answered, and some didn't. The kids got their spiel down after a few houses and got quite good at looking cute, non-threatening, and inquisitive as they tried to get people to agree to take the form to be picked up later. After a few hours, they handed out all the questionnaires they had. They had also taken notes along the way about any people who seemed suspicious. As expected, there were other houses in this wealthier neighborhood with security and gates that they couldn't access. They would have to figure out how to find out more about them later.

Chapter 9

The next day, Hudson arranged his bedroom to serve as their central investigative headquarters. Against one wall, he set up both a whiteboard and a bulletin board from his mom's teaching days, which he had brought up from the basement. Hudson also set up a few extra standing lights so they could see better, and he put a folding table in the middle of the room with three chairs around it. On the folding table, three spots had folders neatly stuffed with paper. Next to those folders were glasses of water and juice boxes, and a basket of little bags of snacks. Against the other wall was Hudson's desk, and on and around it was his computer equipment and toys and knick-knacks, all perfectly aligned and parallel and at right angles to each other, as was his way.

"Ok, please take your seats," Hudson instructed. "In front of you, you'll find a folder that includes a summary of the information we have gathered so far. All the deets in that folder have been sent to you digitally, but I figured having printouts would work better for open discussions." Cai and Sage could tell Hudson was in his element, planning, organizing, and problem-solving. Neither inserted themselves; they let him go like an old wind-up toy.

"The first thing I felt we needed was a name for this operation. In your folders, you will see the code name 'Operation: Middle Finger.'" Hudson smiled wryly at this name. "This is not meant to be offensive; I actually think this is a kid's middle finger," he said as he pointed to the mini-fridge in the corner that now contained the unidentified digit. Both Cai and Sage smiled. Hudson was a wise ass, that was certain to them.

"I got us started in a few ways. First, I organized and collated all the information from your canvassing efforts and then cross-referenced it with my online research into missing children and other incidents of note within the local area." The girls nodded in agreement; they couldn't believe this was the same Hudson, shy, reserved, and only a young teen. This Hudson was confident, organized, and commanding in his leadership. This is a person they could follow.

"Based on this, I have selected the top persons of interest. That's POI to you, laymen," the girls rolled their eyes; they knew what it meant. "In your folders, you will find each one." Hudson put the pictures from his folder on the bulletin board along with a local area map.

"First, it's interesting to note that all of our top suspects and POIs were from the immediate area," Hudson pointed at the map with his pen as an improvised pointer.

"Down the street, just a few blocks away, is our first POI: our family doctor, Dr. Dedorius. Now, I think he is a really nice guy, and I would call him a POI instead of a suspect. Well, at this early stage, we are just trying to find out if a crime has even been committed, so everyone is a POI.

"Dedorius is interesting for a few reasons. First, we should be aware of a national news story about him from about ten years ago." Hudson took the article out of his folder and pinned it to the bulletin board as he read it aloud.

"Doctor and Family Injured In Horrific Car Accident

May 15, 2012, 7:01 AM - On their way home from a family vacation, local physician Doctor Stephen Dedorius, his wife, Susan, and their two children, Macy, 12, and Lucas, 10, were involved in a near-fatal car crash with a semi-trailer truck on Interstate I-95. The police are reporting that the family's car was nearly totaled. The doctor is the only family member not in intensive care, having been spared the worst injuries."

"Is there a follow-up article?" Sage asked. "Did his family survive?"

"Yeah," replied Hudson. "They did, but all suffered serious life-changing injuries. The wife and the two kids have been homebound for the past decade, and the doctor takes care of them. It's pretty common knowledge around town that the guy is like a saint for taking care of not only his disabled family but also all his patients. I think the POI is less about the doctor and more about one of the kids or the mother. People have seen them hanging around the house, but no one ever sees them outside the home or in town or anything. It just seems like something we should dig into a little more.

"The next POI is someone I am sure you both know, media personality Kelly Martin, a mainstay on both Fox and CNN." Hudson pinned an oversized glossy picture of the well-known star on the bulletin board. "It's been a minor news story that she has a child who went missing about a year ago, and so far, nothing has turned up. Like the kid disappeared, and I can't find any follow-up story in the press saying they were found. It just seems weird that the news isn't focused on it. I think it would make sense for us to look into it.

"Our next POIs are a wealthy couple named Bob and Karen. They live just a few blocks away in one of the larger houses in the area. According to my research, several years ago, they lost a child in what was supposed to be a standard hospital procedure. Like Kelly Martin, they are wealthy and exclusive people, as both are corporate executives at a

Fortune 500 company, so we need to be clever in reaching out to them.

"Finally, the one POI that does not seem to be loaded with money and position is the owner of the local CBD store and tattoo shop, The Inner Mind, Nico. A few years ago, he also reported a child missing, so I think it would be good to ask him a few questions about his situation."

"So, what are the next steps?" asked Sage, trying to process what was a new exercise to her.

Before Hudson could reply, Cai did. "We should go back to the houses we submitted the questionnaires to, pick them up, and then maybe ask some follow-up questions."

"Yep, who knows how many people actually filled them out, but we should try," replied Hudson. "When you talk to people, as we have seen on our murder shows, we need to keep an open mind and focus on evidence and data, not supposition and suspicion."

"Ok, so what's the plan?" Sage felt a little left out; she wanted to contribute more, but wasn't finding an area to add to. A part of it was that Hudson wasn't the most perceptive when it came to other people's feelings. In fact, he was downright ignorant of what other people were experiencing at any given time. It's not that he was insensitive or cruel; he couldn't interact with others in the ways they wanted him to. Unfortunately, much of the time, it came off as condescension or aloofness.

The difference here was that Hudson liked Sage very much. He told himself to be patient with her. Hudson thought he was being polite, but Sage could tell he was irritated with her question. She didn't let it bother her. She knew Hudson was unique, and that a certain amount of empathy and sympathy would go a long way toward productive interaction with him. Hudson, of course, was oblivious to all this.

"How about you two go out again and collect all the questionnaires, bring them back, or email them to me, and I will put everything together so we can review. We will then talk about the next steps. Does that make sense?"

Sage and Cai nodded in agreement. They both felt caught up in the whirlwind of Hudson's attention to process and detail. Both girls absorbed his excitement, and in turn, they made him even more excited about their new adventure. The game was on. There was a mystery to be solved, and the Cereal Club would be the people to solve it!

Chapter 10

Sage and Cai spent the next few days knocking on doors and trying to pick up questionnaires. The kids were surprised at how many people actually responded to them. It seems their pleas for patriotism and to protect kids from horrors unknown worked pretty well on the average American adult. They couldn't lap that stuff up any faster; the kids joked to each other on the way home.

Armed with their new information, Cai and Sage returned it to Hudson, who was waiting at Operation: Middle Finger HQ, aka his bedroom. He spent the next few days organizing the combined information and then called a Cereal Club meeting to discuss the next steps. On the bulletin board, Hudson posted some new pictures, along with instructions and other diagrams relevant to the case written out in Hudson's childishly sloppy writing on the whiteboard.

"Welcome, team, to the Operation: Middle Finger strategy meeting. I've been busy, and I know you guys have been too, so thank you for all your hard work." Hudson felt good that he had considered the girl's feelings. In contrast, both girls thought his accolades sounded forced, but were thankful he at least tried.

"If you look at your folders, you will find detailed information on our persons of interest; that's POI for you laymen." Hudson loved that joke and said it endlessly. Sage and Cai, not so much.

"Oh my God, Hud, you gotta stop with that joke," said Cai. Hudson smirked and continued more seriously, not getting that they really did not find a repeated joke funny and really did want him to stop.

"The good news is that our list of primary POIs was reconfirmed with the new data I incorporated into their profiles. A few people are harder to reach, so we will need to establish a separate dedicated op to produce more data on them.

"For instance, media personality Kelly Martin lives in a gated mansion, and she has security, and there is no way we are going to get her to fill out a questionnaire."

"Hmm, how do we get close to someone like that?" Sage asked.

"Well," Cai replied, "a person like that is driven by image and ego. We need to get to her when lots of people are watching. That way, she will be forced to reply to save face publicly." Hudson and Sage looked at Cai impressively; she seemed to understand people without any fluff or B.S., which you usually hear when describing a person's motivations.

"Ok, I like it. Any ideas?" replied Hudson.

"Well, this woman plays herself up to be a big patriot, how she loves Jesus and all that," said Cai. "Oh, and she has her kids' charity that she runs. What's its name again?"

Hudson had already looked it up online. "It's called The Little Angels: Wings of Love Sisterhood."

"Really? Yuck. She sure does love herself, doesn't she?" Cai was making her most disgusted face.

"So that's it!" exclaimed Sage. "We dress up as supporters of The Little Angels. Find out where she will be for some lame in-person appearance, and we ambush her. Wait there and ask her questions in front of the cameras and everyone!" Sage felt good about finally getting in on the conversation, which so far had been totally dominated by the more aggressive personalities.

"It's a plan," replied Hudson. "I'll find out where her next appearance is online. It shouldn't be too tough."

"What do we want to ask her, exactly?" inquired Sage.

Cai jumped in, "It seems like her kid just disappeared. I think we want to ask her if he is an official missing child. Was he a victim of foul play? Or maybe she did something to her kid, and no one knows about it." Cai was smirking a bit; you could tell she didn't trust anyone. "So, let's go light a fire under her ass and make that woman jump!"

Chapter 11

It wasn't difficult for Hudson to find an appropriate event to ambush the celebrity, Ms. Kelly Martin. Her need for public adoration and external approval could never be satiated. This is the curse of all emotionally stunted narcissists who are bound by vanity for their entire lives. While to some, it may seem like their frantic activities are part of a broader outreach to 'give back' to the community and help children at large, any armchair psychologist can tell you they are busy working to give others the false impression of their non-existent empathy.

For the shallow person, acknowledgment of their supposedly selfless activities is the only goal in doing them. The activities they undertake to get that acknowledgment are, frankly, incidental. They will do whatever it takes to fill the empty hole in their heart. For Ms. Martin, filling that emptiness was a 24-hour, 7-day-a-week slog. It never got easier as the years passed, and it never gave her what she was missing—unconditional love and acceptance.

The event was a typical one—a fundraiser for bulletproof vests for police dogs. Never mind the fact that police dogs are horribly abused just by the nature of their forced 'jobs' and die very young due to stress and other medical issues. But getting a bulletproof vest for those poor abused animals will make all the difference in the world to crusaders like Kelly Martin, apparently.

Based on Hudson's online research, Cai and Sage dressed up as what they thought a Little Angel would wear. They wore Little Angel T-shirts, American Flag shorts, and an American flag baseball cap, and both held plastic American flags. Hudson was there to record everything, but he planned to do it inconspicuously so they wouldn't scare Ms. Martin.

Luckily, the event wasn't too far from Hudson's home, in the conference room of a Marriott Courtyard Hotel. They made up an excuse to tell Brody it was for school and have him walk them there. Once at the hotel, they asked random people questions to determine when their target would arrive and where it would be. People were only too happy to talk to these adorable little patriots, who shared a positive message about America and children's rights.

Sage and Cai positioned themselves on the sidewalk where the car was scheduled to drop Ms. Martin off. Hudson sat hidden, a bit separate from them, near a bike rack and behind a bush. Just then, a new white Bentley pulled up exactly where it was supposed to, and out stepped a gorgeous, near-six-foot blond-haired beauty known to the world at large as media personality Kelly Martin.

Surprisingly, perhaps because this was a local event with many cops, she did not have her usual bodyguard detail. As Kelly Martin exited the back seat, she scanned the area, looking for press or cameras. She didn't see anyone off the bat, at least no one that mattered, so she began the short walk from the car to the hotel while smiling, waving, and doing all the B.S. she hated doing. What she doesn't do for charity and kids, she thought.

"Hello, Ms. Martin. May we ask you a few questions?" The sound came from the lower right, which she did not expect, so it startled her a bit. Damn, she thought, what a day to leave the bodyguard home. Now, I have to deal with these kids. Oh well, maybe it will be a good photo op. She then noticed they were Little Angels, dressed in freedom gear and very cute, so she relaxed.

"Why sure, darlings. What are your names?" Ms. Martin bent down only slightly.

"I'm Sage, and this is my friend Cai."

Just then, it became apparent to Ms. Martin that several news outlets and maybe an influencer or two were at the location. They began huddling in when they saw the engagement, figuring it would make good copy. Ms. Martin got a little more nervous; she never wanted to be in an unscripted situation like this. People lose careers this way. Not to worry; what harm could a couple of little girls do?

"Ms. Martin, your compassion and support of children in difficult situations is well documented." They knew buttering her up first would disarm her. "As is your support of critical children's charities like The Little Angels: Wings of Love Sisterhood." Ms. Martin was beaming, and the girls were ready for the kill.

It was Cai's turn to chime in now. "Which is why we are sure it must have been traumatizing when your son, Dylan, disappeared nearly a year ago. Can you provide us with any updates on the status of your son? And how are you holding up?"

To Kelly Martin, it felt like everything had gone into a vacuum as sound and time slowed. Her brain tried to process what had just been said to her in front of the world. How did these kids find out about Dylan? What does she mean by disappeared? Who sent these little shits here anyway? She tried to compose herself.

"Why, how nice of you to ask. I had no idea the status of my child was common knowledge. Dylan isn't missing a young lady;" then, a perceptible pause, "he's been away for a year studying abroad."

Now, it was the girl's turn to be shocked. Nowhere in Hudson's research did they read anything about her kid being in school somewhere, only that he dropped off the face of the planet about twelve months ago.

"Oh, that is so good to hear," said Sage. "You can never trust the internet. Where is he going to school, if you don't mind us asking?"

Just then, as Ms. Kelley pretended not to hear the last question, she waved and smiled at the crowd and hurriedly said, "Thanks so much, everyone! Thank you for coming!" Within a flash, she was off and into the hotel.

Chapter 12

"We're going VIRAL!" Hudson was shouting. Cai and Sage sat right beside him, so he didn't need to yell.

"We are right here, Hudson," Sage said, smiling. They were getting used to Hudson's idiosyncratic behavior and how to react without inviting further provocation.

Based on her cue, Hudson realized he was acting out of bounds and tried to tone it down slightly. "When I say viral, I mean it. We've done over 500,000 views in 48 hours."

"No way!" exclaimed Cai as she got up to look at Hudson's screen. Sage did the same. It was true. Neither had ever seen so many views on a video, and the comments were coming in like wildfire. It seemed people were not too happy with Ms. Kelly Martin.

"My guess is we got picked up by some influencers," Hudson was beaming. "Also, I know at least one local news station picked the story up, as they were right there at the event. Who knows how big this will get if more media covers it?"

"What are people saying?" Sage inquired.

"I'll read you a few choice comments. It looks like the web sleuths are on it, and this woman's dirty laundry is about to be exposed," replied Hudson. "These are all part of a new web community called Where is Dylan Martin? This is from their mission statement on their homepage. They say they are dedicated to using the collective power of crowdsourcing to locate Mr. Martin and ensure his safe return. Ok, here are some comments.

From @steffpicks596, 36 minutes ago: *Where is Kelly's son, Dylan? She doesn't seem very concerned.*

From @bigdadddy1294, 10 minutes ago: *What school is Dylan Martin going to? Why is Kelly dodging this question?*

And from @chunkylover296, 6 minutes ago: *Did Kelly Martin dispose of her son? Where is he? Is he OK?"*

"Holy shit! We got her!" exclaimed Cai.

Being able to hold abusers accountable gave Cai great satisfaction. She had to grow up very young to survive and get by. The degree of trauma Cai had experienced was far beyond the ability of Hudson or Sage to comprehend. As clever as Hudson was and as empathetic as Sage was, they were still innocent and trustworthy children. The illusions of youth and fantasies of tomorrow don't have a place for an individual like Cai, who deals with the ugly realities that others only read about.

"What should we be doing to help all this along?" asked Sage.

"Great question," replied Hudson. "Mostly, we just let the internet do its thing. It will snowball to a certain reach, and we'll get the necessary information. I couldn't have imagined it would have worked this well. If anyone contacts me online about the case, I'll connect with them to build our followers and increase our reach even more. If we get any heat from the authorities or Ms. Martin, we'll play dumb. We are just kids, right?" Hudson was smirking.

All of them felt a real sense of satisfaction that they would be the ones in control of this situation. Control was not a feeling most kids got to experience, especially those in toxic home environments.

Over the next few days, the video continued to go viral, eventually hitting close to 1.5 million views. When The Cereal Club returned to school on Monday, their street cred improved considerably. Before the video, they were either ghosts in school, never acknowledged, or the subjects of humiliation and abuse. But now, they were regarded with pleasant curiosity or given props by some other students. It turns out it feels pretty good not to be a social pariah 24/7 and have some support from the people around you.

Chapter 13

The viral growth of the 'Where is Dylan Martin?' video changed things considerably for Hudson, Sage, and Cai. Firstly, it turned them from nonentities at their school and in their town into somewhat minor celebrities. Eventually, the video reached almost 2 million views. Still, more importantly, it sparked an internet research movement similar to the ones that have found missing children and solved murder cases around the country.

The 'Where is Dylan Martin?' web group found Dylan within a few weeks. Finding the truth only took several hundred web sleuths and a few dozen hours of searching and investigating. It turns out that about two years ago, Dylan, like millions of other young people, was infected with the COVID-19 virus. Like a significant percentage of the people who get it, he developed Long COVID and was left disabled. Now bedbound and unable to walk, Dylan had become an embarrassment to his high-profile celebrity mother. How could a leading media personality, trusted by viewers of FOX and CNN alike, have a son disabled by a virus that is no big deal? Ms. Martin needed to do something with him, and she needed it done quietly.

So, in the dark of night, about a year prior, she had him committed to a mental asylum: The Golden End Wellness and Holistic Retreat. She completed the necessary paperwork, and nice men in white coats arrived in no time to forcibly remove Dulan from his home. Dylan was held against his will, without the ability to communicate with the outside world. This is where Dylan had been hiding for the past year. All doped up on psychiatric meds and kept in a locked hospital room, not allowed to use his phone or talk to his friends, all so Kelly Martin could protect her reputation and career.

The Internet sleuths found this documentation online pretty easily, from the initial diagnosis to the paperwork for commitment. With this information, just like the 'Free Britney' movement that preceded it, a 'Free Dylan' movement was sparked, which was dedicated to freeing the young man from his abusive mother and her control over him. A petition to Free Dylan was circulated online and eventually garnered over a million signatures. Free Dylan supporters were showing up in the background on TV shows and news programs, with signs and chants constantly calling attention to FREE DYLAN!

As one can imagine, the negative press for Kelly Martin was devastating. It turns out Americans don't like celebrities much when they find out who they really are. First, Ms. Martin tried to ignore it. She told the press and public that this was a personal family situation, and it was rude and invasive for people to think they had the right to know. She was indignant that her character was being questioned. But, as more information came out online, her tone and manner changed. Once reporters asked her about where her son was committed and about his diagnosis, she became like a deer in headlights. Ms. Martin then went into hiding, and within 48 hours, her hiatus from both FOX and CNN was announced. Within a week, her podcast had been canceled, and major advertisers had distanced themselves from her failing brand. It turns out Ms. Martin was right to be concerned, as unscripted interviews can only lead to bad things for the synthetic, inauthentic celebrity.

Once Kelly Martin's business and image were destroyed, there was little reason for her to keep Dylan locked up in a mental wellness retreat. In addition, her funds were drying up, and she couldn't afford to keep him there. But it turns out Dylan no longer wanted to live with his mother. Apparently, a mother abandoning her son for her own convenience doesn't go over well with that individual. Luckily for Dylan, he was now over 18. But he was suffering greatly from the effects of Long COVID and could not afford to take care of himself.

Once again, the internet group 'Free Dylan!' came to the rescue. They started a crowdfunding campaign to raise enough money for Dylan to get his own place, acquire some healthcare, and free him from the clutches of his narcissistic mother. Within a few months, over $2 million was donated to his FundHe account, and Dylan was given a new lease on life, no thanks to his mother.

His mother got her comeuppance. Kelly Martin's career was destroyed, and her reputation was in tatters. Her image was all that mattered to her, and once that was gone, all she could do was attempt to regain it in any way possible. Within one year, top-tier media personality Kelly Martin was doing ForFans.com nude modeling to pay for what was left of her lavish lifestyle. Eventually, she began dating washed-up '80s child actor Corey Feldman and was dumped by him when she, ironically, got Long COVID herself. The cycle was complete. She was spit out of the bottom of the entertainment industry, eventually getting so much plastic surgery that she was called an unrecognizable cat lady in the popular entertainment publications of the day.

Chapter 14

All the hubris surrounding the 'Where is Dylan Martin' movement distracted The Cereal Club from its primary mission, Operation: Middle Finger. Hudson, who valued digital life far more than IRL, now had more online friends and connections than ever before. His whole digital world had opened up to include thousands of people. It didn't fully occur to Hudson that these new people were acquaintances at best, not actual friends.

Cai and Sage were now considered cool by the school's popularity set. Guys and girls constantly inquired whether they wanted to go to this birthday party or that one, and what their weekend plans were. Sage, who was so outgoing and empathetic, reveled in this new attention, increasing her friend group by the day.

Cai had a different reaction. She had been around the block and knew that fair-weather friends were just that. They were only there when times were good. As soon as things went sideways, they would look for greener pastures. Cai knew that her friendship with Sage and Hudson was authentic. It was based on communication, understanding, and respect, not on trite issues like how someone looked, how cool their parties were, or how much money they had. So, Cai treated all her new 'friends' with the same skepticism she treated everything.

About a month after the Kelly Martin scandal, Hudson reconvened the Operation: Middle Finger meetings. Frankly, it was the first time they had been together at Hudson's house in a while, with Sage being pulled away more and more by her new group of friends. Cai kept hanging out at

Hudson's house after school, watching murder shows and playing games, as was their way.

It took some time, but Hudson finally worked up the guts to ask Cai what it meant when the neighbor kids were bullying her. "Seriously, Cai and I don't mean any disrespect," Hudson asked demurely, "but what's up with those kids ranking on you? I mean, is it some racist insult or something?"

Cai could see that Hudson was genuinely confused. "Fine, I'll tell you. But I swear to God, if you start messing with me about it, I will kick your freaking ass." Cai stared Hudson down, who cringed under her cower, and then she softened up a bit when she felt bad.

"Well, it's about what my real name is. My mom is kind of a free-spirit type, you know? Well, she gave me a dumb name, and I don't like it. Because of what you saw, people make fun of me for it." Hudson could tell this really bothered Cai.

Cai looked around to make sure no one was lurking in the shadows. "My full name is… Coyote. Get it. Whoo-hoo!" She did her best wolf impression. Then she tired of it quickly. "So…a few years ago, I changed it to Cai. Like Cayote. Coyote. I don't know, whatever." She was already getting irritated talking about this stupid name that was so far into her past at the ripe old age of fourteen.

Hudson finally got it. Not that he would have ever figured it out himself. Coyote to Cai? Maybe Cay or Coy? But that sounds like a fish. Well, whatever. He could certainly see why she wanted to change it to reduce the schoolyard abuse. What is it with parents, Hudson thought? They constantly tell you and the world how selfless they are, and then they give you a name that they think is cool but makes you a target for every bully on this side of the Mississippi.

"Ok, I got it." Hudson backed off quickly, not wanting to get a rise out of her. This is where Sage was needed. They both missed Sage. She was so positive and supportive. She added some necessary warmth to the relationship that both Hudson and Cai lacked.

But today, all three members of The Cereal Club were present and focused on the task at hand. As usual, Hudson was firmly in charge, having prepared a new set of folders for each member, each containing their next POI. As was his way, Hudson put out snacks and drinks for everyone. Also, as usual, Hudson's room was immaculate, with everything on the tables perfectly parallel and at right angles. Right before the beginning of any meeting, Hudson would walk around the room, straightening everything and putting things in their place so that real work could begin. If anything was askew, he felt he could not concentrate and would be forever distracted by the disorder around him. He was constantly tidying and ordering his immediate universe.

"Welcome back to the reconvened Operation: Middle Finger strategy session." Hudson smiled and thought it was the funniest thing ever whenever he said the ops name. The other two members of his team, not so much. Hudson's repetitive jokes were just that, repetitive. Neither of them said anything to him, though. Why take away such a small pleasure from him?

"I am sure I can speak for us all when I say the results of our first mission were a resounding success," he continued. "Sure, we did not get closer to finding our missing child without a finger, but we did eliminate a major POI. And Ms. Martin, while not guilty of a crime as heinous as murder, was an awful person who needed to be held accountable for her behavior."

Cai had a big smile on her face. "You got that right, Hud. This woman was a PoS, plain and simple. And guess what? There is no system, no police officer, and no adult who will hold someone like her responsible. The system is there to protect people like her, not hold them accountable."

Sage and Hud just had to agree. They knew Cai knew more about how adults really thought and behaved than they did. She was considered an expert in this area.

"Well, I figure we got Dylan free from his imprisonment, so we did the right thing," said Sage. "But I won't revel in someone else's pain and suffering. I'm not saying she isn't a bad person, Cai; I just don't think it's good for us to enjoy her pain."

Cai kind of smirked, thinking she understood what Sage was talking about, but she hadn't a clue. That level of empathy didn't exist for her. Her life has been too harsh. Hudson tried to understand Sage's point of view, but he fell more on Cai's side. He didn't have the same level of empathy built in as other people did.

"Well, I think we can all agree we did our job here and did it the right way," Cai responded. "We can't control what the media does or how the general public reacts. I mean, it was her choice to commit her only son to an institution against his will! And with her being in the public sphere, there would be repercussions for her behavior. All we did was make the world aware of Ms. Martin's true self. I don't see any issue with that."

Sage didn't let her friend's inability to empathize with others fully bother her. She knew that something lacking or damaged in each of them didn't permit that same level of insight into their own behavior. Sage had patience and sympathy in droves.

"Ok," said Hudson. "Everyone is making some good points." Hudson was trying hard to provide some form of leadership to the group, and he had read that making positive, reinforcing comments like this helped people feel good about themselves. "Let's move on to our next POI, or POIs if that is more appropriate." Hudson looked around for someone to smile at his joke, but no takers, so he moved on.

"Up next in your dossiers is our local physician, Dr. Dedorius."

Each folder had been updated with a large color photo of the doctor on the front. Inside each folder were all the details about him, his home and work, and the last known pictures of his family.

"As a refresher, the doctor and his family were in a really bad car accident a little over a decade ago. The doctor, his wife, Susan, and their two children, Macy, aged twelve, and Lucas, aged ten, collided with a semi-trailer, and they all went to the hospital with life-threatening injuries. The doctor got out of it the best, with minor physical injuries, but his family was all hurt severely, and they have been homebound for the past decade. So, word around town is he works his butt off to take care of his family, along with all his patients. Basically, the guy is like a saint."

"So why are we investigating him?" asked Cai.

"Well, we are trying to find out whose finger that is. Maybe it's one of his kids? No one has seen them in years, so how do we know something didn't happen there?" replied Hudson.

"All right, make sense," said Sage. And then, after a quick thought, "You know, I have a checkup scheduled with him next week."

Hudson's ears pricked up. "Really? That's great. Sage, do you mind asking some questions during the exam to probe him a bit? Then Cai and I will case his house and try to dig up some more information."

"What are you thinking, Hud?" Cai's eyes were twinkling.

"Hmm, some light recon to start. Eyes, ears, phones. Then, we can dig a little deeper. I've got some ideas," Hudson replied.

Chapter 15

"Turn your head, please," the doctor said, looking through his eyepiece and examining Sage's inner ear. "So, Sage, how is your mother doing?" He was always so considerate, thought Sage, and he looked just like a doctor should, too. With gray hair and a white coat, he proudly displayed all his awards and certifications on the wall.

"She's fine, doctor. Thanks for asking," Sage replied. She had to remind herself she was there to investigate and ask questions. She needed to be as objective as possible.

"How's your family doing, doctor?" That was a good segue, thought Sage.

The doctor was taken aback for a moment. Few people asked him how HE was doing. Actually, no one ever asked him about his family. This inquiry quite touched him.

"They are doing very well, Sage. Thank you for asking," the doctor said with a big smile. "How considerate of you." He always tried to reinforce good behavior in his younger patients.

Sage thought that wasn't enough; she needed to get more out of him. "How old are your kids now?"

"Well, let's see," the doctor was busy and seemed unsure, "they are in their early twenties by now. I'm unsure if you're aware, but they both still live at home with my wife and me." The doctor looked down, and Sage could tell she had hit a nerve. This poor man loses his family, but does not entirely lose them. He has to work to take care of them in their disabled state while still working a full-time job and keeping up appearances. Sage saw the pain in him and the love for his family. At that moment, she couldn't imagine this man harming any member of his family for any reason.

"I'm sorry, doctor, I didn't mean any offense."

"No, no, Sage, don't be silly. You have nothing to apologize for. The truth is that my family and I suffered a horrible car accident about ten years ago, and while we survived, my family was forever impacted. Now, my beautiful wife can only stay home, and she helps me take care of our two lovely children, who are also homebound."

Sage wanted to cry. She felt so much compassion for this man. "Oh, doctor, can I do anything to help?"

The doctor looked at her warmly. "Sage, just keep being you—so decent, sweet, and considerate. That is all you need to do to help."

While this touching display was going on down the street, Hudson and Cai approached Dr. Dedorius's residential home. Like other higher-end houses in the area, his yard and driveway were gated, making it challenging to approach unnoticed. The good news was that it was a corner lot so that they could see the house and yard from some distance down the street, from multiple angles.

Since it was the middle of the day, Hudson and Cai decided to stroll down the sidewalk while checking out the house. Hudson had his phone set to record audio so he could take notes and was ready to take a few inconspicuous pictures if possible. As they approached the house, they heard a lawn being mown. The hum of workers grew louder as Hudson and Cai rounded the corner to see a group working on the lawn of the Dedorius home.

At first, Hudson was inclined to retreat, but Cai didn't waver, so Hudson just kept walking along with her, as planned. They engaged in pointless chit-chat while paying close attention to everything they saw and heard. If there were anything to note, Hudson or Cai would insert it into the flow of their inane conversation so it could be transcribed by Hudson later.

The workers paid little attention to the two kids, and the kids paid little attention to the workers. The house was in good condition, as one would expect for the home of a moderately wealthy doctor in a respectable upper-class community. It was larger than most on the block, was white, three stories, and had well-developed trees and a lovely stone border fence.

"Pretty nice," mumbled Cai. "I mean, if you are going to be stuck somewhere like this family is, it isn't too shabby."

"Do you think the family is only stuck indoors, or can they be out in the yard?" Hudson wondered aloud.

"Huh. Good question, Hud." Hudson literally blushed at any compliment from Cai.

During the daytime, there wasn't a ton to see. The lawn workers were busy at work, and the house seemed quiet. They found a larger tree and leaned on it, mostly out of view of the workers.

"Hud, check out the garbage they already put out. Maybe we can rifle through that later and look for clues?" Cai whispered, pointing to the neatly packed garbage and recycling canisters near the driveway.

"I love it," Hudson replied. "I can't see too much through their windows, though. And we can't approach the house with these gates. Even if we jumped over the walls, we would be too visible." Hudson was silent for a few seconds. Then it struck him. It was so simple. How couldn't he have thought of it before?

"Holy shit, Cai, I've got a badass idea."

"And what idea is that, Hudson?"

"Brody got a drone for his birthday this year. It has HD video with night vision, image stabilization, and everything. If we are careful and return at dusk, maybe we can do a little aerial recon. What do you say? You think you can go home a little late tonight?"

Cai nodded in the affirmative. "Believe it or not, my mom told me she would pick me up a few hours late, so it's not a problem."

"Great, let's go back to the HQ and set up Brody's drone, hopefully without him noticing, and come up with a plan." Hudson was getting all amped up. Cai loved it; she was getting caught up in his excitement. Heck, she had to be honest with herself; this was fun. And not to be at home, that was even better.

Chapter 16

Back at the house, Hudson got dressed in darker clothes and lent Cai a dark blue hoodie. After a short search, Hudson found Brody's drone and ensured it was charged. He put it in an oversized bag, and they snuck out while Brody was on the phone. It wasn't hard to get things past Brody, as he clearly wasn't paying much attention to them.

After arriving at the Dedorius home, they found a large tree near the side of the house. After laying the drone on the ground for takeoff, they climbed up. As soon as they settled into the tree, a late-model Mercedes pulled up to the front gate, which opened.

"Wow, just in time. It looks like the doctor just got home," Hudson said.

The doctor pulled his car into the garage, and within a few minutes, he walked back out with something in his hand.

"And look at that—he's putting the garbage out," Cai said as the doctor stuffed a smaller garbage bag into a large green can. He then rolled the can onto the street for pickup in the morning.

"Boom," said Cai triumphantly. "Now we just wait a bit, and I will go down and fish that bag out." The second the doctor closed the garage door, Cai jumped and moved stealthily from the tree to the front gate. Luckily, no one was around on the street, so she could easily lean into the can and grab the plastic bag. She then stashed it in a bush near the tree where they were hiding. Within a few seconds, she shimmied back up the tree, all silent and stealthy.

"Where did you learn to move like that?" Hudson asked her, totally impressed.

"Hud, when you live in the area I live in, you learn to move quickly and quietly." Cai didn't look at Hudson when she was talking.

"I'm sorry, Cai." Hudson didn't really understand, but he knew his friend was hurting. He quickly changed the subject to the business at hand. "All right, please watch out for any passersby. It's getting dark enough to use the drone without it being too obvious, but if someone is looking right at it, we can't hide it. Just give me a heads up if you see something, and I'll hide it from their view." Cai nodded her head. She had highly tuned senses and was the perfect lookout.

Hudson started the drone and, using his controller, slowly began moving it vertically. He kept it near the big tree they were in while going straight up. Once Hudson had the drone near the tip of the tree, parallel to the house's roof, he moved the drone closer to the home. Cai kept an eye out and saw no one walking down the street. Any cars that passed never saw them as it was dusk and difficult to see.

Once the drone was near the house's roof, Hudson slowly moved it down the side to get a look into some of the windows. Hudson felt bad knowing they were doing something he knew was wrong by spying inside a private home. The club had discussed this at length, and it was decided that bending the rules to do that was acceptable since they were trying to solve a serious crime. But all Hudson wanted to do here was confirm that the doctor's family was well and were not victims, and that was where it ended. He would not look into anything beyond what he was here to do.

When the drone approached the second-story window, Hudson had the video and audio recording, and the night vision turned on. The shades were drawn, but he could make out the shadow of a man, most likely the doctor himself, milling around the bedroom, apparently getting ready for dinner with his family. Hudson could hear him talking to someone.

"Honey, where are my night-time PJs? You know I like to wear them when I get home." The doctor talked loudly to his wife, who was probably preparing dinner. "Oh, wait, I found them, sorry! I'm coming down now."

After that, Hudson scanned the rest of the second-story windows with the drone and, seeing no activity, began lowering it so he could check the rest of the house. As soon as he got down to a first-floor room, he could hear the sounds of a regular family having dinner together.

First, he heard the background noise of several children talking and laughing in the form of inane chatter only kids can fully understand. He kept moving the drone sideways until he came to what was the kitchen and dining room. The shades were drawn, so he could only see shadows and movement, but he could make out the outlines of two children sitting around the kitchen table.

Just then, the doctor entered the kitchen and, with great fanfare, went to where his wife was preparing food and hugged her. The doctor then kissed each of his kids on the head and sat down to enjoy a meal with his lovely family.

At that exact moment, unknown to Hudson and Cai, a concerned neighbor saw the drone hovering outside the doctor's home and called the police. Unfortunately for Hud and Cai, a patrol car was right around the corner, and in an instant, flashing lights and sirens raced up to the house. Cai reacted first, having been in this position before, and screamed at Hudson to 'RUN!' as she launched herself out of the tree and ran at top speed through some hedges and into the night.

Hudson was utterly shocked by the whole experience. He had never 'run' from the cops or anyone else before. There had never been any reason to. He knew he would get in big trouble for spying on someone's house with a drone. He had to get rid of it, along with the controller. So, when Cai took off, instead of trying to run with the massive drone, he sent it up vertically and landed it on the doctor's roof, hoping the police wouldn't see. Then, he left the controller on the top branch and climbed down. The cops were pulling up just as he dropped down. They pointed their lights at him, and Hudson had nowhere to run. He was busted.

Chapter 17

"What were you doing up in that tree?" Two huge cops towered over Hudson as he sat handcuffed in police interview room number one.

"I was just tree climbing; I'm a kid, you know." Hudson had seen enough true crime shows to know how this worked. The police would bully and browbeat him until he gave them the information they wanted. He knew they were legally permitted to lie to him, and he could not trust what they said.

"We climbed up that tree and found what you stashed," the smaller of the two cops said. Hudson was pretty sure that was a lie to trick him. He didn't see the cops go up the tree after him, and he doubted another set of cops went there after.

"I didn't stash anything in the tree, officer," Hudson knew to be polite but not to give an inch. These cops wanted to incriminate him, not help him. He tried not to sound too snotty, but he didn't talk to adults the way most adults thought kids should. He spoke to adults like they were his peers because, frankly, intellectually, they were. Adults did not seem to like that at all, especially those who thought they were in a position of unquestionable authority, like the police.

This mouthy fourteen-year-old kid caught the cops off guard. He was way too obstinate for a child his age, and he talked too intelligently and world-wise for his years.

Hudson had an ace up his sleeve, as he knew police were not permitted to hold him and question him without a lawyer present. At any time, Hudson knew he could ask for a lawyer, and the police were legally required to stop their questioning. Hudson had noticed that the vast majority of people who were convicted of crimes in true crime shows did not exercise their constitutional right to legal representation and permitted the cops to interrogate them. Forget that the cops weren't supposed to be interrogating him anyway, without a legal guardian present. He was underage.

The cops decided to change tack. "Look, son, we got a report from a neighbor that someone was flying a drone and peeping in people's windows. So, we pull up to the area and see you and your friend jumping out of a tree, and one of you running away. You understand this looks suspicious. Now, why don't you tell us what you were doing up there?"

"Seriously, officer, my friend and I were just running around and playing after school. We thought it would be fun to go tree climbing. Some of us kids still go and play outside, you know. We got scared when we saw the police car, so my friend ran. I'm really sorry about that." Hudson put his head down and looked at the ground, acting contrite and submitting to their superior authority. Whatever made these goons leave him alone was fine with him.

It worked somewhat on one of the cops. You could tell he had kids and was more sympathetic than the other. "Who was your friend, son?"

Hudson didn't even need to think about it. He would never, under any circumstances, rat his good friends out to anyone, especially the police. "I'm sorry, officer, but I can't divulge that information. I would be exposing my friend's identity without her permission."

Both cops were gobsmacked. They weren't sure how to deal with this…child. Was he for real?

"This isn't a request, son, it's an order. Tell me who your friend is, NOW!" The meaner cop leaned in, getting in Hudson's face. He was actually spitting a bit, getting Hudson's glasses wet. Clearly, he was trying to intimidate this young child physically. Hudson wasn't having it. He didn't flinch.

"I'm afraid I cannot do that, sir." Hudson was petrified, but he wasn't going to show them. He took his microcloth out of his pocket and cleaned his glasses calmly and steadily. He remained staid.

"Listen, you little shit, give me your phone and tell me your password, RIGHT NOW!" The meaner cop was bright red and about to lose control.

Hudson knew he had better be careful, or this cop would smash his head into the desk. Think being a kid will protect you from these goons? Think again. "Officer, I am truly sorry for upsetting you." This seemed to piss off the cop even more, having this brat tell him he wasn't in control. "But I simply cannot give you my phone without a warrant or probable cause. Any good lawyer would tell their client never to provide that."

The nicer cop leaned into the meaner cop and whispered a bit. Then the nicer cop said, "Young man, we are concerned you are hiding some important information from us. We think you should do a lie detector test to confirm you are telling us the truth."

Hudson wasn't surprised at all. This was police procedure 101. If they couldn't browbeat him into a confession and bully him into giving them access to his phone, they would go for the traditional anti-science chestnut, the polygraph.

"I don't think I would feel comfortable submitting to a polygraph officer," he said with confidence and conviction. Both cops were bowled over.

"Excuse me!" The mean cop got aggressive again, pushed Hudson back into his chair, and shoved him against the wall. 'Why would you not want to do a lie detector? What do you have to hide?"

Hudson was no sucker like these police were used to dealing with, "Sir, can you please not spit in my face?" Instinctively, the mean cop backed up a bit. "I have nothing to hide. First off, there is no such thing as a lie detector. Period. No such device has ever been invented. A polygraph measures changes in body physiology; it is not a lie detector. Second, polygraphs are not admissible in most courts. That's because they are quackery and are not scientifically valid. If they were real science, they would be admissible in court. Third, you can lie to me about the polygraph results, so I have no way of knowing what those results were. And regardless, they are interpreted by a biased polygraph examiner who can, in fact, lie to me about the results as he sees them."

The officers were speechless. Even if people were aware of their rights, which they rarely were, they never had the nerve to say them to the cops' faces. They usually just demanded a lawyer, if anything. Few Americans whom they interviewed knew what a load of crap lie detector tests were. The whole true crime genre primarily works to justify the cop's bullying tactics on a suspect or person of interest. Its role is to convince regular people that there was this thing called a lie detector and that this quackery device could legally be used to bully people into a confession, false or real. That is all the lie detector is. Pseudoscience is deployed by a state-sanctioned body like the police and district attorney departments to force confessions from people under manufactured circumstances. There is no science involved, just intimidation. Any lawyer will tell you, under any circumstance, to never submit to a polygraph, ever. It is only beneficial to the police and the prosecution, not anyone else.

After another brief chat between the cops, they decided this was a waste of their time. Besides, it was almost time to grab a drink, so they certainly didn't want to be doing any paperwork on an obnoxious kid.

"Get out of here, kid," the nicer cop said, unlocking Hudson's cuffs.

"And you better listen up. We know you now, and if we catch you climbing up trees and peeping in people's houses again, it won't end well for you, understand?" The meaner cop barked at him without even looking Hudson in the eye, dismissing Hudson as the non-entity he considered him to be.

Hudson knew he won, this round at least, and he flew out of that chair faster than he had ever moved before. He was out of the front door of the police station and was turning the corner when he heard a sound from the bushes.

"Hey, Hud."

Hudson knew right away it was Cai. He slipped into the bushes to talk to her.

"Are you OK, Hudson?" Hudson could see the look of concern in her eyes.

"Oh yeah, I'm good. They tried to intimidate me, but I didn't budge."

"I'm sorry I ran, Hud. I didn't want to abandon you, but I couldn't let the cops get me."

Hudson knew that Cai would not abandon her friend. She got away from the cops but watched them take Hudson to the station and waited outside until they were done interrogating him.

"I know that, Cai, you did right. I did not rat you out to them, that you can be sure of."

"Thanks, Hud. I know I can count on you." The two kids were right. They could count on each other. On other adults and authority figures, not so much.

"The problem now is that Brody's drone is on the doctor's roof. We will need to figure out how to get that back, hopefully, before Brody figures out it's gone." Hudson realized he wasn't out of trouble yet.

Cai nodded her head. "We'll figure it out, Hudson. Look, the good news is we can cross the doctor off the POI list; he seems like a decent guy doing his best to raise and take care of his family."

"Agreed," replied Hudson. "Let's return to my house so you can go home; we're not too late. Then we'll work on the next POI in our investigation."

"You got it, Hud." Just then, to Hudson's total surprise, Cai hugged him—a real hug. Like a hug of thanks and friendship, and it was something Hudson had never experienced before. Real compassion and empathy from another human being. He almost melted from the genuine expression of

love he had never felt before. He didn't know how to hug
back, so he just sat there and accepted it.

Chapter 18

"Are you OK, Hudson?" Sage looked concerned as Hudson and Cai told her about their encounter with the police.

"Yeah, I'm fine; what a couple of assholes, though," Hudson replied, trying to act tough, but he was still scared. He never had to stand up to bullies like those two cops, and he did it all alone, without any adult present. It didn't matter to Hudson, though; he knew if they called his father down there, he would have sided with the police, no matter what they said or did.

"You should have seen him; he didn't flinch when they grabbed him." Cai was positively enamored of how Hudson stood up to the cops. "And this tough little homeboy didn't even rat me out." She leaned over and gave Hudson a big hug and a kiss on the cheek, and Hudson blushed and was uncomfortable but appreciative. Sage was pretty amazed by how close the two of them seemed now. And she was, if she was honest with herself, a little jelly.

"Yeah, well, before they got me, I felt bad about spying on the doctor. From what I saw, he seemed like a stand-up guy. I was ready to move on when they pinched me," Hudson reflected.

Sage was nodding in agreement. "Oh, I agree. Dr. Dedorius is so sweet and decent. He's compassionate, and he cares."

Cai didn't say anything. She knew better than to trust people based on a few shallow interactions. But she didn't see any reason to disagree with them. They didn't find anything to change the doctor's status from POI to suspect, so he should be removed as a POI.

"Well, we do have one problem with him that still needs to be resolved," Cai inserted.

"Yep," said Hudson. "Brody's drone. It's up on the Dedorius roof. I can get the controller stashed in the tree no problem, but getting that drone back will take some planning. Brody hasn't used the drone in a few weeks, so let's hope he does not notice it's gone before we can replace it."

Cai and Sage nodded, unsure how they would get on the roof to retrieve the drone. But, they had more important things to do, and an active investigation into a child's missing finger needed to be prioritized.

"Let's move on to our next case, for now, guys. If anyone gets any good ideas on the drone, we'll discuss it and make it a side mission. Who knows, we may need the drone to investigate our other POIs." Hudson handed out a new set of folders with their next persons of interest, Bob and Karen, corporate executives. The image showed a well-groomed middle-aged couple: the man in a blue suit and the woman in a floral-patterned dress, with big, expensive-looking chunky jewelry.

"Damn, that's a good-looking couple," Cai remarked.

"Well put together, too," inserted Sage. "You can tell they have bucks."

"Oh yeah," acknowledged Hudson. "According to my online research, these are two top corporate executives with Lyzer Pharmaceuticals. He is the Chief Financial Officer of one of their divisions, and she is the Chief Marketing

Officer. According to financial filings, they both have compensation in the millions. However, like all corporate executives, their salary is for PR and tax purposes. They make all their real money from stocks.

"I did some research, and here is how it works. Their companies reward them with profit-sharing compensation like stock, which is taxed much lower than people's salaries. In the business world, this is called capital gains tax, and if you want to know what rich people care about, it's capital gains tax. Since rich people make all their money from investments, not actual work like normal people, they make sure they are taxed much lower than everyone else."

"That doesn't surprise me, Hudson," sneered Cai.

"For instance," Hudson continued. "My dad, a contract laborer, gets taxed at about 30% of his salary. A rich person who makes money through investment is taxed from 0-20%."

"So, the game is rigged?" asked Sage.

"Oh yeah, fully rigged from the top to benefit the rich at the expense of everyone else," Hudson said as Cai nodded aggressively.

"Well, we are not here to condemn the system but to find out what happened to a child who is missing a finger. This couple has a bit of a shady past regarding their own kid, which puts them on top of our POI list. I would say they very much approach suspect territory.

"Let's do a quick data dump on them. Based on my research, they are big Democratic supporters and donate to local, state, and federal campaigns. They supposedly have very close ties to Hillary Clinton, with the wife hosting various fundraisers to support her causes. You know the type - bullshit causes. They are subscribers to the New York Times and the Washington Post, and his wife regularly leaves comments on The Huffington Post and online places like that. It's all pretty typical liberal elitist behavior, staying within the lines painted for them and never veering off the path. Looking at this couple from the outside, they are successful, good-looking, healthy, compassionate, and do all the right things. Well, all the things expected of them in our society.

"Let's see what else? They own nice cars, as expected: a Mercedes for the wife and a BMW for the husband. Like many business people, they travel on business about 90% of their time, so they exist mostly in that corporate world. Everything they do is connected to their corporatist lifestyle and worldview. It's all about how they get promoted in their jobs and compete with other corporate people. They are careerists. Image matters to them as it does to someone like Kelly Martin, but their image is less about abject vanity and more about conformity. Bob and Karen are the kind of people who need to fit in no matter what. This couple says and does everything right when someone else listens or watches." Both Cai and Sage were stunned by Hudson's depth of information gathering and his ability to make sense of it all and connect the dots for them.

"So, why are they on our list? Well, according to the news and my online research, a few years back, this picture book couple had a beautiful young daughter who was about our age and went in for a standard medical procedure and mysteriously died. From what I can find in the papers, they could never determine CoD; that's Cause of Death for you amateurs." Hudson looked around for a smile and didn't get one. Maybe this joke was getting old? Nah, he thought, it was still hysterical. "The death was mysterious, which is why they are our next POIs. As I looked into their financial history and career information, and after their child died, both of them saw a huge increase in their compensation and positions. Now, maybe they both threw themselves into their jobs and became even more successful after the death. Or maybe there is something else going on we need to look into."

Sage and Cai were on the edge of their seats. Hudson was like an eloquent thirty-year-old lawyer during their meetings. "Hud. When you say the daughter died mysteriously, what do you mean?" Cai was pointing at a picture in the folder, the most recent of their daughter, Isabelle, from a year before her death.

"Well," Hudson was cleaning his glasses, for the umpteenth time this day, "according to the local paper, the kid went in for a routine medical procedure. Then she somehow dies in the hospital, which is bad, right? Well, it gets worse. The parents don't ask for an inquiry into their child's death, and they don't sue the hospital or doctor. The issue is buried and disappears from the news quickly."

"What kind of parents don't want to know the details of their child's death?" asked Sage, horrified and disgusted. "And what kind of parent doesn't want to investigate it and hold the appropriate people accountable?"

"That is the question, Sage." Hudson was getting amped up again. "This doesn't pass the common-sense smell test. Either these are terrible people, which they very well may be, or there is more to this story than we are being exposed to."

"Yeah, but this is a tough one, Hud." Sage was deep in thought. "How do we get that information on the child and the hospital?

Just then, a light went on over Cai's head; you could almost see it when the idea struck her. "Holy shit, you guys! My Mom is a part-time nurse at that hospital. I mean, it's one of her three jobs."

"Your Mom works three jobs?" Hudson was shocked; he didn't know people did that. Why would anyone want to work three jobs? How do they sleep, eat, and do other things, like play video games?

"Yeah, Hud. People around where I live either work three jobs or are on the street; it's that simple."

That blows, Hudson thought. He wondered why people put up with such poor treatment. He also wondered if they had a choice.

Sage spoke up. "Cai, do you think your mom can help us?"

"Well, like any other adult, she won't take us seriously. But I thought it may be a way to get in there and poke around a bit." Cai suddenly had a great idea. "Oh, I know; I can ask my mom if I can come to work with her for a day, you know, like kids going to their parents' work day. I bet she would love that."

Hudson and Sage were giddy. Hudson spoke first, "Cai, that would be amazing. I think it would be just keeping your eyes open, maybe asking a few pointed questions here or there. If you can arrange to spend a day with your mom, I will get to work on the computer in the next week or so. See if I can find out more about this couple and why they would not want to look into their daughter's death."

"What about me, Hudson? What can I do to help?" Sage really wanted to play a role in this phase of the operation.

"Great question, Sage. We need to understand these people and how they think. How do you think we can learn more about them?"

Sage didn't hesitate to reply, "My family and their culture are very spiritual and, well, in regards to the finger, have a background in similar areas." Hudson had no idea what she was talking about.

"So yes, I would be happy to look deeper into the family and the situation regarding the finger." Sage felt relieved that she had some role in this endeavor. She knew she had something special to bring to the investigation, and it was about time she ensured they were a triad, not just two with a sidekick.

"Great," Hudson said. He was satisfied that they had not only a productive meeting with concrete steps, but that he hadn't offended either of his two friends. He was rather proud of that fact.

Chapter 19

Hudson spent the next few days at his computer researching Bob, Karen, and their daughter Isabelle. Like many techies, Hudson built his desktop computer from the ground up. This was called a 'rig' by gamers, and this was a fully decked-out tower model with see-through glass and flashing, color-changing LED lights on the fans. Hudson also used a mechanical keyboard since he loved the clicking sound and feel of the keys hitting. The keyboard he used was also LED-lit, which, along with everything else, gave his room a creepy, futuristic glow that all gamers seem to love.

At this point in his life, Hudson was starting to get into listening to music while he did things. He didn't have a lot of older people to influence him musically, so he was influenced by what he heard on the internet and during TV shows and commercials. He was already getting into classic rock, as there didn't seem to be anything too recent that Hudson connected with. Today, Hudson was rocking out to the song "All Right Now" by the English blues rock band Free. It was the first time he heard it, but it sounded like he had already heard it a million times.

"All right now, baby, it's all right now…" Hudson had no sense of tune. He was off-key and humming and singing to himself, and he couldn't have cared less what he sounded like. Damn, he thought, this music is pretty badass.

His research was going well. The good news about public companies is that they are legally required to submit certain information to the state. For instance, Hudson could tap government resources, such as the Patent Office, to track the products certain companies make. Doing online research was more about knowing how to search for things digitally than breaking into something. Yes, there were hackers out there who could tap into confidential healthcare files, but Hudson wasn't a criminal. He could get what he needed through legitimate means.

While Hudson was progressing on his assignment at home, Sage was moving forward with her task. While Hudson was the product of his environment and who he was born to, so was Sage, but her history was very different and deserves some highlighting.

Sage was, unlike Hudson, an actual native American. A real native American, meaning her people were living here when European colonizers came over and violently stole their land during what we now incorrectly call the Discovery of the New World. When the colonizers couldn't force people like Sage's family into subservience and slavery, they imported millions of enslaved Black people from Africa to run their plantations and steal the native people's resources. Many native people then ran from the coasts or were forced out and had to make their way into the interior of the jungle of South America, or they would be enslaved or killed by the invaders. Almost all of the native peoples surrendered to the conquerors or joined them in an attempt to save themselves and their families. But there was one tribe, one group, who never gave up. One people, who in all of the Americas, never surrendered to the colonizers. The Shuar people, from what is now called Ecuador and Peru.

Before the Invasion of the Americas, the Shuar lived and fought for their homeland for thousands of years, as ancient cultures have done since time immemorial. In the year 1599, instead of submitting to the invading Spanish demands for gold and forced slave labor in their mines, the Shuar destroyed the Spanish settlements in which they were imprisoned and liberated their people from colonial rule, for a time. In reality, the Shuar continue to suffer from colonial and corporate encroachment into their rightful lands to this very day, forcing many to relocate around the world.

The Shuar gained notoriety in Western society as the South American tribe known for practicing headhunting. That is, they practiced ceremonial beheading, known as tzantza, of their enemies to procure their spirits and use them for their own tribe's benefit. This is important to be aware of, since it is this particular cultural skill set that Sage wanted to discuss with her father, Karakras, a Shuar shaman.

In her bag, she carried the finger she took out of Hudson's refrigerator, with his permission. "Father, I've brought the item we talked about. Would you mind taking a look at it?" Sage was excited for some attention from her father, not only because he was typically very busy but also because she knew this was his specialty. She knew he would have wise and thoughtful insights.

Karakras looked up from his desk, shifted his mind from work to his daughter, and smiled, "Ah, the cute one." He doted on his child when he could. "Have you come to learn of our culture?" He nodded his head towards the box she held.

Sage smiled back. Her father was a traditional man who was educated in the ancient ways of his people, but he also had a heart and loved his daughter very much. She knew this and could forgive his other limitations due to his embrace of her through unconditional love.

Sage proceeded to tell her father all about the background of the missing finger, from the day the cat was dropped off at their house, to their attempts to bring it to the police, and their investigation of suspicious neighbors. Like any kid, she was smart enough not to tell her father the whole story. So, she omitted the info on her friends spying on the doctor, but included the police's poor treatment of Hudson.

Karakras had been around the block more than a few times, and he knew he was getting the rosy 'we did nothing wrong' version of the story. But he was proud of his daughter for taking the initiative to show compassion and support to another human being, whether or not she knew that person personally. Her self-directed action and personal accountability at a young age were something to be proud of.

Karakras let his daughter finish her story; he did not interject or interrupt but showed her the respect she deserved as a human being and allowed her to speak her truth. Once Sage was done, he spent some time in thought before responding. All his words were weighed heavily and deliberately. He opened the box and thoroughly examined the finger, with all his expertise in Shuar traditional practices.

"Sage, you have brought to me a mystery. But one that we can surely gain deeper insight into. When our people practiced the ancient art of creating tzantza from the bodies of our slain enemies, these were not simply trophies, as the colonizers like to assume. We sought the muisak, or, as Europeans would call it, the spirit or soul, which we believe resides in the head. With that, the hunter would gain control over their enemy's wives and daughters and their labor to make food and beer. As Shuar women cultivated the land, Shuar men believed their female ancestors would bestow good crops, which is why taking tzantza was so important.

"I do not see a trophy when I look at this finger. I see something much deeper, for it is connected to a mystery I do not fully comprehend. I can tell you that, on examination, this finger was removed deliberately. It was not cut due to disease or damage, nor for sport. It was cut for a different purpose; one I cannot fully discern now."

Karakras spent a few moments in reflection. Sage knew to be very quiet and not disturb her father's meditations. "Sage, this is not a simple matter. I must use the sacred cup and the sacrament of ayahuasca to enter into a visionary state and discern the reality behind this mystery. I will enter into penke karamprar with the deceased child."

Sage was shocked. Going into an ayahuasca trance to obtain visions was no light undertaking. But penke karamprar was something different. That was when the traveler's spirit visited the spirit of a deceased friend or relative. She had never heard it being done for someone who wasn't closely connected to the traveler.

"Father, I did not wish to impose such a responsibility on you."

Karakras only shook his head. "No, child. The act of the child being violated was what imposed a responsibility on me as a shaman. The visions will guide me to seek justice and peace for this victim. I act as an interpreter, not a judge."

Sage was satisfied and knew not to occupy her father past her inquiry. She hugged him.

"Sage, it will take me some time to prepare and understand the visions."

"Of course, father, thank you for everything." Sage quickly departed her father's office while he returned to his work.

Chapter 20

Cai walked with her mother, La'Shell, into The Old Springs Community Hospital for her mom's second job, Assistant Nursing Supervisor for the night shift. Before entering the emergency room entrance, Cai's mom turned to her and handed her a child-sized KN95 mask.

"Put this on, honey; you don't want to go in there unmasked." Cai didn't question her mother; she knew her Mom cared about her and was looking out for her best interests. She put on the mask without argument.

Upon entering the emergency room waiting area, Cai noticed it was packed, with people coughing and sweating everywhere. As they walked through the ER, the hallway was packed with patients on gurneys, many with oxygen tanks attached to their faces. Everyone looked pale and deathly ill. Cai was alarmed.

"Mom, what is going on here?"

La'Shell replied in a quiet voice under her breath, "Honey bunny, we are in year five of an ongoing pandemic, that's what is going on."

"But I don't get it, Mom. I keep hearing that it's over."

"Take a look around this hospital. This pandemic has gone nowhere."

"Then, why are we the only ones wearing masks?" Cai really didn't understand the logic of 'post-pandemic' America.

"We mask not just to protect ourselves, but to protect the people around us that we love, like grandma. We don't want to bring any germs home to her, right?"

"Of course not." Cai felt angry that anyone would mess with her defenseless Gran Mama.

"That's right, honey," La'Shell looked at her intently. "We do what is right, no matter what everyone else does or says. It's like that old Bob Dylan lyric, 'You don't need a weatherman to know which way the wind blows.' Common sense decency is just that."

They eventually arrived at La'Shells' office, which was little more than a converted broom closet with a desk and a computer. Once inside, her mom got Cai settled in a chair and found her a small-sized nurse's outfit. With her uniform and mask, Cai's mom thought she looked adorable. How lucky she was to have such a strong, independent daughter. She did worry about what her daughter had to endure to be so resilient. As her mom, she did her best. There is simply no way to be an effective parent while being worked to the bone as a wage slave for subsistence pay. There is only survival and maintenance, no growth or development. La'Shell wondered if that was part of the point. Keeping her and her family so busy and poor, they could never challenge the rich people who were screwing them over.

Cai was supposed to be at the hospital, ostensibly to learn about her mom's job. But she was really there for an ulterior motive, and that was to find out all she could about corporate executives Bob and Karen and the mysterious death of their only daughter. At this point, Cai wasn't sure how to do that other than keep her eyes and ears open and ask some innocent 'I'm just a kid' type questions. She knew adults love to talk about themselves and their jobs, and it was all about just asking the right things to get them chatting.

"What can I do to help Mom?"

"Well, honey, I'm going to do my rounds, check in on the nurses, go over schedules, things like that. How would you like to come with me and take notes?"

"You got it!" Cai grabbed her mom's work tablet and took her phone in case she needed to take pics or record anything for her other assignment.

Cai and her mom spent the next few hours walking through the hospital's various floors and departments, performing the daily duties of an Assistant Nursing Supervisor. It mainly consisted of double-checking nurses as they did their rounds, filling out digital forms, and going through checklists. All the nurses loved Cai in her little nurse's outfit and commented on how cute she was. Cai found it all pretty revolting but played along; she knew what adults wanted to hear and see.

All that most adults want to see in their children is their reflection, and they imprint their desires and needs onto their kids to see that happen. This is what many adults call nurturing: an attempt to force their persona and ideals onto a child. Cai was her own person; she didn't need any adults to imprint themselves on her. She was as independent and self-assured as any grownup.

After the early evening rounds, Cai and her mom got something to eat in the hospital cafeteria, and it cost them almost $50 for two cheap, mass-market lunch items.

"Holy cow, Mom, is this how much you spend to eat every day?"

"Haha, no way, honey, I bring my food from home. I figured we would have a little treat because you were with me today."

Cai felt special knowing her mom went out on a limb for her like this. She knew that money was a big deal to their family. "Thanks, Mom, I really appreciate it." She gave La'Shell a big smile and nod, instantly making her mom feel better. After dinner, Cai and La'Shell returned to her office closet, and her office phone rang while La'Shell was busy doing computer work. "Hello. Oh, sure, no problem. I can get that for you. Just give me a few minutes, ok?"

After she took the call, she turned to Cai and said, "Honey bunny, I need to get some information from the basement. But I have to get these forms done. Can you go down for me and get this?" La'Shell was writing down some notes on a scrap of paper and handed them to Cai.

Cai was excited. An assignment! And a chance to do a little investigating. "You got it, Mom. Where do I need to go exactly?"

Cai's Mom shot her a little coy look and said, "I'm afraid it's the morgue you need to go to, sweetie."

Cai acted like it was no big deal, but she was kinda freaked out. She had never been around or seen any dead bodies before. She didn't know what they would smell like. Gross, she thought. Cai's Mom could see the apprehension on her child's face. "Are you sure you can handle it, baby? I can do it later after I get this paperwork done." La'Shell knew precisely what to say to Cai to get her engaged.

"Cai toughened up immediately. "No, I got it, Mom, not a problem. Just head down to the basement, huh?"

"Good luck! Oh, wait, here is my master key; it opens any door in the hospital. Only use it for the morgue if needed, OK? But don't worry, there will be an attendant you can talk to."

"Done and done." Cai ran out of the room like she was free for the first time in her life.

Chapter 21

The creaky elevator kept going down. Lower-Level 1…Lower-Level 2…Basement-Level 1…Basement-Level 2. The doors opened slowly, and Cai stepped out into a dimly lit hallway with flickering fluorescent lights and bulbs that had not been replaced in some time. She could see years of accumulated grime down here that didn't seem to be in the rest of the hospital. It was clear this was a low-traffic, low-priority area.

There wasn't another person around, just a dingy yellow hallway stretching to the left and right. There were two signs on the wall: one pointing to the left, labeled "Morgue," and one to the right, labeled "Records Archive." Cai turned to the left and walked down the hallway, which eventually turned again. Towards the end of another dimly lit hall, she came to a door labeled Morgue, and in front of it was an empty desk. The desk held some papers, a small laptop, an empty cup, and a sign that read "Morgue Attendant."

Huh, thought Cai, this must be the guy my mom wants me to talk to, so where is he? Cai took out her phone and checked her messages and updates for a minute or two while she waited for the attendant to return. After about five minutes, Cai was getting impatient. She looked at the note her mother had given her, which said, "Get information on recent morgue entry. Name, ID number." Huh, that seemed pretty straightforward. Where was this guy? After a few more minutes, Cai was concerned her mom would be getting worried about her. Should she return with nothing or try to get the info herself? Cai looked down at the master key she had, and she realized she could go in there, get what she needed, and be on her way.

What the heck, she thought, I may as well check inside and see if I can get what I need. If I don't see anything, I'll go back upstairs. Cai built up her confidence, pushed the master key into the Morgue door lock, and clicked the door open. The click was so loud in the silent hallway that Cai almost jumped out of her shoes. She slipped into the doorway and felt the wall for a light switch, which she found. She clicked it on.

The morgue was a white-tiled room with empty metal tables or gurneys lined up in nice rows. It was lit by ancient fluorescent lights that gave everything a creepy white-and-yellow glow. A central table in the middle looked like the place where examinations were held. Along one wall was a series of metal doors where bodies were held in a refrigerated state so they did not decompose. Some of those doors were partially open. Cai had seen a few rerun episodes of The X-Files before at Hudson's house, and this looked just like the morgues she saw in that show.

Most of the room was clean and not occupied, except for one table in the back corner. She could see a plastic body bag covering what she assumed was a corpse, with a paper tag hanging off it. Well, thought Cai, that is probably the information I need. But that body was all the way on the other side of the room, and Cai did not immediately go to it. She was frozen in place; her legs would not move. Cai had never been frozen in fear, so this experience was new to her.

She knew the faster she did this, the sooner she could leave this room. As she walked over to the body bag in the corner, everything seemed to go in slow motion. She could hear every step echoing off the metal tables and tile walls.

The lights flickered, almost seeming to be in sync with her steps. With each step, the lights flickered off and on. On and off.

It seemed like ten minutes before she made it to the body, lying prone on the metal gurney. The tag hanging off the bag's zipper probably had all the information she sought. So, Cai took out her phone, turned on the camera, and went to grab the tag. As she did and turned the tag sideways to read it, she accidentally unzipped the bag a bit, and the wafting smell of decomposing flesh hit her in the face. She winced at what was probably the worst smell she had ever smelled. Like many emergency responders will tell you, it was a smell that you never forget.

Cai decided she had had enough of this adventure, and it was time to go, so she quickly took a picture of the body bag tag. Just as the phone camera clicked, Cai felt a cold whiff of air from behind, making her shiver. As she was about to turn around to see what it was, a hand touched her shoulder, and Cai screamed and jumped about two feet in the air.

"Young lady, what are you doing here?" The man wore a white coat with a name tag that said "Morgue Attendant."

Cai tried to regain her posture. "Sir, I am so sorry. My mom, La'Shell, asked me to come down and get some information from you. I decided to come in and get it when you weren't here."

"I was on break. But that doesn't mean you can unlock doors and go wherever you want," the assistant said, irritated. He wasn't as irritated as he would be if he were actually on an official break, but he wasn't.

"Yes, sir. I am sorry to bother you." Cai turned quickly and
ran down the hallway, vowing never to return to a morgue
again.

94

Chapter 22

Cai ran out of the morgue so fast she didn't notice when she made a wrong turn on the way to the elevator. She began to panic when it became clear she wasn't anywhere she had been before. When Cai stopped to catch her breath, she was in an even more unmaintained part of the basement. It was even darker and grimier than the morgue, if that was possible. In front of her was a door, and a sign on that door read, 'Archived Records Room.'

Cai had to process it for a moment. She wondered if she could get some information on Isabelle and her parents here for Hudson? If there were any confidential information that wasn't digitally protected, it would be here. And as luck would have it, she had a master key to the hospital. She decided to try it and see if it worked. She slipped the key into the lock and turned it, and it clicked. She opened the door slightly to feel for a light switch inside. She found it, turned it on, and went inside.

The room smelled of musky old paper that had been too damp for too long. Rusty-looking file cabinets lined the walls, and metal racks with cardboard file boxes made up rows in the middle of the long room. The room went into the distance, and Cai couldn't pinpoint where it ended. If Cai thought the morgue was freaky, this was scary as shit. At least in the morgue, living people came in and out. It looked like no one had been in this room forever. If something happened to Cai in here, would anyone ever find her? She wasn't supposed to be here. Maybe her body would decompose like the one in the morgue, and if the smell got bad enough, perhaps someone would find her then.

Cai shook off the creeps. The faster she did this, the quicker she got out of there. She knew the surgery date from the newspaper article and Isabelle's last name. So, Cai started walking down the aisles, trying to discern what system was used to arrange the information. Lucky for her, the files were arranged alphabetically by year. So, she found the year 2015, and there was Isabelle's backup medical record. Cai planned to take pictures of each page of the file with her camera, but she noticed the file was pretty hefty. It would take her some time to take all these pics.

Just then, there was a click, and more light came into the room from the now-open doorway. Then Cai's hair on her arms and neck stood up in terror. She immediately jumped behind a metal file cabinet to hide.

"HELLO!?! Is anyone here?" a maintenance worker's voice boomed into the dank room. He had noticed the light under the door, and no one ever went into the archived records room. When there was no reply, the worker assumed someone had just left the light on, turned it off, and closed the door.

Cai was left in pitch black, her heart thumping, and sweat forming on her lip. What should she do now? Wait? For how long? She didn't want the worker to see her coming out, but she also knew it was too long to get back to her mother; she would soon get worried.

Cai waited about five minutes. Those were five of the longest minutes of her life. Sitting in the black all alone, holding onto the files, hearing squeaks and creaks from God-knows-what in the darkness. She could feel her pulse thumping out of her neck with every second that passed by.

Finally, Cai turned on the light on her cell phone, went to the door, and peeked out into an empty hallway. When she saw no one present, she ran out of the room, still holding the files, past the morgue, where the attendant was out front, down the hallway, hit the elevator button, and returned to the populated floors. She vowed never to return to Basement-Level 2.

Chapter 23

Cai delivered Isabell's medical file to Hudson the next day. It was so thick and complicated that she barely looked at it. She knew Hudson would use his superior problem-solving abilities to make sense of it and connect it to the rest of the information they had researched.

She was right. Hudson spent the next few days compiling and cross-referencing information that he had gathered online with her medical file, and he was able to create a compelling narrative of what happened to poor little Isabelle. The information Hudson had found was explosive. He was prepared to present his findings to his investigative partners but knew he had to step up his presentation game to connect the dots for them.

Hudson had been saving his birthday and holiday checks to buy a digital projector for his cell phone. When the girls came over after school for their weekly check-in, Hudson had set up the table with updated folders and photos. His new projector now sat in the middle of the table. It was projected on the whiteboard with a PowerPoint placeholder slide that read, Operation Middle Finger: Bob, Karen, and Isabelle. Of course, Hudson put out a bowl of snacks and drinks for the team, as was his way.

"Nice digital projector, Hud." Cai nodded at the new device.

Hudson was visibly proud of his new tech. He LOVED technology and gadgets. Each piece he acquired, he felt, added something to his own being and persona. They gave him something to focus on and something to care about.

For Hudson, focusing on and caring about people wasn't always possible, so tech and hobbies were his primary ways of engaging with the world and others.

"Welcome back, team." Hudson seemed excited, and Sage noticed. He must have found something good.

"As you can see, my energy is very high right now. First, I want to congratulate Cai on getting Isabelle's archived medical records from the Community Hospital. This was incredibly fortunate, but it would not have happened if Cai had not taken the initiative and been in the right place at the right time. So, nice work, Cai.

"And Sage, I know you talked to your father, and he is going to look into our situation and the source of the finger. We look forward to hearing more about that. Thank you both." Hudson felt he was being appropriately empathetic. He checked whether both girls looked satisfied; they seemed OK, so he moved on.

"I spent the last few weeks digging up information on Bob and Karen, along with what Cai dug up on Isabelle. And let me tell you, this was some interesting research." Hudson could see the girls were on the edge of their seats. "I'm going to walk you through what I found."

"First off, let's talk about what happened to Isabelle at the hospital. According to the records, she went in for a standard procedure to heal a minor bone fracture. Then, she dies on the table. Weird huh? It gets weirder. Guess what her CoD is? That's Cause of Death for the amateurs." Hudson looked around for a response and didn't get one.

"Well, her CoD was determined to be 'natural causes.' Yes, you heard that right: a twelve-year-old kid goes in for minor outpatient surgery for a bone fracture and dies from natural causes. Wow." Both Sage and Cai were shaking their heads since no kid dies from natural causes. She didn't die of old age, that was for sure.

"OK, so we have a kid dying on the table, and the hospital calling it natural causes. It seems like a cover-up for the hospital's negligence. The real question becomes, why didn't the child's parents sue the hospital or file a police report and hold them criminally accountable?"

"They don't seem like very good parents to me, Hud," Cai sneered.

"Well, well, Cai. You would be right. Now, we get into the nitty-gritty. Both Bob and Karen work for the biotechnology pharmaceutical company Lyzer, right? Both of them were mid-level managers before their daughter's death. Well, after their daughter's death, they were both promoted almost instantly to C-suite positions with huge stock packages. Quite the coincidence, huh? Well, it looks like it is not a coincidence at all."

"Tell us more, Hudson." Sage was sipping her drink, munching on a few snacks.

"Ahem. So Lyzer manufactures a painkiller called NoxyRotin, which is used for outpatient surgery. It's supposedly considered a less addictive option than other opioids. According to the medical records Cai absconded with, Isabell was medicated with Noxy, which, according to my research, has a high probability of overdose when used on children under sixteen years old. So, the doctor doing the procedure there should never have prescribed it to her. While there is no direct evidence that she did OD from this drug, what else did she die from if not that?

"So, Isabelle most likely dies from the same medication that her parents' company manufactures. The only way to know if that was true would've been to do an autopsy. Well, guess what? According to the records, the parents denied the autopsy. Apparently, they did not want to know what happened to their daughter if it implicated their company or impacted their careers. They chose not to do an autopsy, decided not to sue the hospital, and chose not to alert the police to possible criminal negligence on the part of the hospital. That is quite extraordinary behavior for parents who supposedly loved their child.

"Of course, the rub comes in when both parents see their careers skyrocket AFTER they decide not to look into the mysterious death of their daughter from the medication their company manufactures. Within a few weeks of the death, they are promoted and given multi-million-dollar stock option packages. It is obviously a payout or compensation for declining to investigate the incident.

"Now, all this is conjecture and is circumstantial at best. The way to truly find out what happened to this child would be to do the autopsy that was never done." Hudson looked at both the girls seriously, wondering if they knew what this implied.

"Jeez, Hud, are you talking about exhuming her grave?" Sage was shocked; nothing could be more offensive to her beliefs and people than desecrating someone's resting place. Her father would not be pleased.

"Well, we obviously wouldn't do anything like that. I mean, we would need to convince the police that there was a potential crime here and have them investigate by testing the body for residual chemical traces. They would need to be the ones to exhume the body and complete the investigation."

Cai was shaking her head. "Come on, Hud, you know and I know the cops couldn't care less. They will laugh us out of the station if we go to them. Or worse, they will hold us, interrogate us, and rat us out to our parents. You can't trust the police, Hud, period."

Hudson nodded his head in agreement. "Understood, Cai. But maybe we can, um, encourage the police to look into it."

Sage was intrigued. "Like how, Hudson?"

"What do the police hate more than anything?" He looked around for acknowledgment but didn't get any. "Bad publicity! That is why they focus on high-profile cases for rich people and ignore pretty much everything else. And if rich people don't want cases looked into, the police are only too happy to accommodate, as long as they don't get bad PR. So, in this instance, a kid dies in the hospital, and it's determined to be natural causes. There's nothing for the cops to do unless the parents push it as an issue. The cops don't want to make it an issue anyway. So, they leave it alone."

"I'm getting what you are saying, Hud," Cai said, furrowing her brow, thinking hard about how to force the police's hand. "We want to elevate this issue as we did for the Dylan Martin situation. No one cared or looked into what was going on with Dylan until thousands, or even millions, of people became aware of it. It took the online crew of true crime advocates and researchers to dig into the issue, and they used their platforms to elevate the message to a broader audience. It seems like we should follow a similar path here. What do you guys think?"

Sage was nodding in agreement. "All we are talking about here is putting some information that should have been public before the public now. This child deserves some justice and acknowledgment of her suffering. And if her parents are not prepared or willing to do that, then we will." Hudson and Cai nodded in agreement; this was about doing what was right, plain and simple.

"OK, I like it." Hudson was all amped up. "I am going to start putting together a website and mailing list, and then I will blast out an alert to all our followers. We need to produce a video or something so people can grab onto it and make it go viral. Let me think about that. Guys, give me a few days, and I will put some ideas together and have them ready to review during our next check-in meeting!"

Chapter 24

Hudson was getting better at working with digital tools, and the quality of his presentations, images, and video to support his storytelling was improving daily. He knew that, for this operation to be effective, he needed to tell an engaging story that would emotionally resonate with people.

It was easier for 'Where is Dylan?' since Ms. Martin was a huge celebrity. People naturally wanted to know about her personal life, and since she had so many haters, people also wanted to bring her down a notch or two. However, in this instance, the POIs were corporate executives who were unknown except in corporate circles. Now, perhaps when a Fortune 500 CEO sleeps with a twenty-something underling, that will make a minor news story, but not much more. It seems all corporate executives are protected under the umbrella of the massive corporate entity to which they are beholden.

As the centerpiece of his campaign, Hudson set up a webpage with a story-oriented layout, leading visitors through a series of pictures and text narratives that explained the case. The page was called: Get JUSTICE for Isabelle! Hudson wanted to generate ire with the general public, so they would call the local and state police to demand action. The page began with an adorable picture of Isabelle, then showed her parents, the hospital, and the operating doctor. All with text below each picture explaining the situation, why the child was there, and what might have gone wrong. It was step-by-step and very easy to follow.

Hudson then showed a picture of Lyzer's pain medication, NoxyRotin, followed by a promotional video claiming it was not as addictive as OxyContin. Following that, Hudson posted a large-scale medical study showing that Noxy should never be used on children under eighteen since there was a high potential for overdose. Finally, Hudson made a video starring The Cereal Club, in which they dressed up in adorable pro-America outfits, with little flags and T-shirts that said JUSTICE for Isabell with a picture of her on the front.

Hudson had figured they would need some revenue to support their various ops, so he offered custom t-shirts for sale on his website, along with bumper stickers and coffee mugs. He sold most of it for a little more than cost, as he had no intention of profiting from someone else's misery. In the video, Hudson, Cai, and Sage, with tears in their little eyes, plead with the public to get justice for poor Isabelle and not to allow this heartless corporate entity and their sociopathic minions to deny the truth from coming out. Only you, the public, can make the police do their jobs and investigate this thoroughly. Did Isabelle overdose on Noxy? Who is responsible? Why wasn't her death investigated? Why don't her parents seem to care? Why did her parents get promotions after her death?

With the video, Hudson submitted it to Younoob and Instasham and alerted his now sizable audience and connections to their new objective. He ensured everything linked back to the main webpage so he could narrate the whole story. Also, on that page, he made sure to include all the police contact information so that online armchair true crime detectives could contact them and prod them to do their jobs. He wasn't sure he could get this to go viral like their other video, but Hudson had built a significant online following and was confident he could get some attention for the issue.

He was right. It didn't explode immediately like the Dylan thing, but it grew a little slower and more organically. Now that Hudson knew people online with significant followings on various social platforms, they helped get the video, images, and webpage address out to a sizable audience. Hudson created shareable social media tiles and graphics with the taglines "Get JUSTICE for Isabell," "Does NoxyRotin Kill Kids?" and similar messages. They played up the anti-corporate angle over focusing on the parents, since they weren't sure anyone did anything wrong until the cops did an autopsy. That was the primary goal of the Justice for Isabel Social Media Campaign, as Hudson had coined it. He would allocate the few dollars they had received in donations to pay-per-click media campaigns in addition to their more direct promotional efforts. Hudson was quickly becoming quite the digital marketer, learning how to get his message out there and get people to support his cause.

After a few weeks, they had received thousands of downloads of their video and driven several thousand visitors to their website. They were selling the T-shirts too, at least a few dozen a week. Based on Hudson's correspondence with other amateur true crime investigators, they let him know that a steady stream of phone calls, emails, and text messages had been sent to the Old Springs Community Police Department over the past few weeks. Hudson was pretty sure that was not enough to light a fire underneath the cops' asses. So, he kept at it. Slowly building traffic to his webpage, pushing his social media tiles out, and promoting the video they created.

During the next operational check-in meeting, Hudson confided in Sage and Cai that the cops weren't taking the bait. He was pretty sure it was because the criticism wasn't public and was delivered over the phone in private. As Hudson has previously commented, the police care about

PR and image, so they needed to make this more public if they wanted action.

"What about a protest?" Sage's eyes were glittering. "We make some signs, wear our t-shirts, and stage a protest in front of the police station and the hospital. Stand out there for a day or two, take videos and pictures, and get the material in front of people through our social media contacts. If lucky, a blogger or local news station will pick it up."

Hudson and Cai were instantly excited. Cai spoke up first, "That is a fantastic idea, Sage. Oh man, that will piss the cops off!"

Hudson was smiling, too. "The hospital won't like it either. Oh, I have an idea too. What if we get people to protest the HQ of Lyzer? Say their painkillers are killing children."

Sage loved it. She nodded. "Do you think we can get people to do that? It's not local and isn't something we could do personally."

Hudson was thinking, "I'm not sure. I need to chat with people and get the concept out there. I can tell you people HATE pharmaceutical companies like Lyzer. They manufacture life-saving medications for pennies on the dollar and then charge sick people thousands of dollars for the same meds to gouge them for money during their most vulnerable moments. I think people will want to hold a corporation like this responsible for potentially killing a kid and then covering it up.

"Team, let me start building a plan. Cai and Sage, can you guys work together to start making the signs and other items we need for a multi-day protest? I will network online to get people to participate. Can you both work with people locally to get them involved?

"You got it, Hud," Cai replied, looking at Sage, who nodded in agreement. "We are on it."

"Thank you, team! Let's get justice for Isabell; she deserves it."

Chapter 25

Within a couple of weeks, the protests were ready to go. They were scheduled for a weekday during rush hour to ensure as many passersby as possible would see the message at multiple locations. A hashtag called #JUSTICEFORISABELLE was made and shared across all social media platforms to get people to rally around it and share it organically. All the protest signs they made, with various slogans, also had the hashtag at the bottom, which helped connect the messaging campaign across real life and digital. All of this was supported by paid advertising, which Hudson funded through donations sent to the webpage and from their T-shirt sales.

The protests were organized into three camps. The first was at the local police station, led by Hudson and Cai, while Sage and some of her school friends led the second protest at the hospital. Finally, the third protest was out of state at the Lyzer headquarters and was led by some of Hudson's internet friends. All Hudson had to tell people was that it was a protest against Lyzer and their pain medications, and people were signing up online like crazy. It turns out that hating Big Pharma was a national passion for many Americans.

About a dozen protesters showed up at the police station, and a similar number at the hospital. The Lyzer HQ saw more, maybe twice that amount. All the leaders were instructed to record the speeches and chants, as well as any problems they encountered. The goal was to livestream them or post them online quickly, to create buzz around the hashtag. All the protesters were instructed to be on the street or in public areas in front of the buildings so they couldn't be arrested for trespassing. At least, they hoped they wouldn't be. It seemed lately that it was illegal just to complain in the USA, with college kids and others being beaten and arrested just for expressing their opinions.

The chants were fun and meant to be memorable. Gems like "JUSTICE NOW! LYZER OUT!" and "HEY…HO…DON'T LET ISABELL GO!" and the crowd favorite, "NOXYROTIN MAKES YOUR BRAIN ROTTEN!".

The protest at the hospital went without incident. Sage and her friends set up, gave a few speeches, and took snaps and videos, all with wide-angle shots intended to make it look bigger than it actually was. Sage's protest was more focused on the hospital itself, the fact that Isabelle died during a routine procedure, and that she was given a painkiller that was questionable to give to children safely. As was agreed beforehand, she kept their activities on the sidewalk in front of the hospital to reduce the chance of police intervention. Her protest overall had a nice hippy vibe, as one would expect from Sage, with lots of hugs, love, and stuff like that. Who would hassle some cute young girls looking for answers to another youngster's untimely demise?

The protest at the police station was a little more intense since Hudson and Cai were leading it. Their event was more focused on getting the police to do an autopsy and find out whether Isabelle overdosed on NoxyRotin. The police were smart enough not to confront the kids directly, but Hudson and Cai could see them peeking out the windows from time to time. Lots of JUSTICE FOR ISABELLE! and AUTOPSY NOW! signs and chants were done. They made sure to include the police station sign in the pics and videos, and to put the police hashtag in posts along with the #JUSTICEFORISABELLE tag. Hudson was clever enough to include the Old Springs Community Police

Department logo in his social media posts, linking their department with this uninvestigated case. Soon, all over the internet, this upper-class, small-town police department was now known to hundreds of thousands of people, as was the unfortunate case of Isabelle's mysterious death.

The protest at the Lyzer HQ went down very differently from the two relatively tame affairs in Old Springs. It turns out that protesting in an upper-class small town in front of a few municipal buildings didn't get the same reaction as mixed-race protesters complaining about corporate America in a large city. The protesters at Lyzer were a bit older and more anti-corporate than the local protesters, which in turn led to a darker situation.

Within a few minutes of the protesters showing up in front of the HQ, Lyzer sent out security guards and agent provocateurs, who are security agents secretly dressed up as protesters, to hassle and bully people. Security began by telling them they were on private property, even though they were on the public sidewalk. The agent provocateurs tried to start fights with the real protesters and caused damage to the property. Security was getting even more aggressive and beginning to push the protesters around when the police showed up. Many of the protesters were relieved that the police were now there to protect their Constitutional right to gather and complain. Boy, were they wrong!

The cops were dressed in full riot gear, with body armor, helmets, and face shields. They were armed with clubs, pepper spray, and other forms of 'non-lethal' incapacitants. They quickly surrounded the several dozen protesters. The group was given no warning as the police began converging on them, kettling the protesters into a small corner near the building. The police then forcibly zip-tied and arrested anyone who submitted. Multiple cops with clubs beat anyone who did not submit peacefully. After the entire group was tied up, they were put into an armored personnel carrier to go to the police station to be arrested for trespassing and disturbing the peace. The protest lasted about 30 minutes, until they were swept off the street without a trace, before any news station could report. Well, anyone but the Cereal Club and their online network, who had the whole event shot on video and uploaded it before the protesters were at the station.

Chapter 26

'WE DID IT! They're doing an autopsy!" Hudson was beginning to like the feeling of success. It was something he had never known before. Being able to do things with others and feel like he was part of something was a truly incredible feeling. Not only was he part of something, but he also felt like a leader in it.

Hudson projected the local news story onto the whiteboard from his phone. The headline read: POLICE TO DO AUTOPSY ON GIRL WHO DIED 10 YEARS AGO. The gist of the article was that the police had been inundated by phone calls from citizens about the potential overdose of a child in the care of the hospital. And because they want to see justice done, even though they think nothing will come of it, the police will be performing an autopsy. Nowhere in the article were any of the protests mentioned. No major media outlet anywhere picked up the protest story. Only some bloggers and true-crime podcasts called it out, giving it life online, but not to anywhere near the level of the 'Where is Dylan?' movement. But it was enough to get the police to do their jobs, which was the whole goal. Cai and Sage wanted to pat Hudson on the back, but neither got the impression Hudson liked to be touched too much, so they just smiled at him and gave him some air-fives.

"Hud, I'm not going to lie; I'm concerned about the people who got busted at Lyzer," Cai interjected, not to take away from Hudson's success but to address an important issue.

"I have to agree, Hudson," Sage said, nodding. "We asked these people to do something for us, and they got beaten and arrested. What can we do to help them?"

"I hear you guys." Hudson knew their part in this, but he didn't have Cai and Sage's built-in sense of empathy. It was behavior he had to learn as he went along, whereas for others, it was innate. "I guess I didn't realize protesting a large public company in a big city would put people in harm's way. It's not like they were doing anything illegal."

"Pfft," Cai was sneering, "that doesn't mean squat in this country. All you need to do is be the wrong color, or not have enough money, or speak truth to power, and the police goon squad will come to crack some skulls. It's literally what they are there for."

Hudson and Sage didn't have a retort to that; it seemed obvious to them that the police were there to benefit the rich, not regular people. Getting them to do things for the public good was about maneuvering them against their will.

"Hudson," Sage was looking at Hudson empathetically, trying to communicate to him how important it was to help others who helped you. "Can you speak with the leader of the Lyzer protest and see if we can help them?"

"Of course, Sage." Hudson understood from Sage that this was important, which was enough for him, even if he didn't fully get it.

Hudson proceeded to pull up his email, and within a minute, he received a reply, "Whew! Guys, he tells me everyone was released within a few hours of their arrest. They were told they would all be prosecuted for trespassing if they protested in front of Lyzer again."

"But, Hud, they were not trespassing; we made sure of that," Cai sounded pissed. She was leaning forward in her chair.

"Yup, as we see, the actual law doesn't apply if they want to target you," Hudson replied. "The law bends for whatever goal authority wants to achieve. The cops want the protesters quiet and off the streets so they can't embarrass rich people on their way to brunch. Period.

"But look, guys, this is a huge win! The autopsy is being done, and the protests and call-in campaign worked. And while some of our friends got roughed up, they are all now free, and nothing will be on their records."

Sage and Cai figured that was a pretty positive outcome after all. Sage said, "Hudson, can we at least send that group a thank you from us for helping and putting themselves at risk? It's the least we can do."

Hudson nodded in agreement. "Yes, I can do that." He quickly jotted off a text and then a group email. After that, he posted an update on the 'Get Justice for Isabelle' webpage about what happened during the protests, thanking everyone, along with info about the autopsy. He told his followers that as soon as the police updated them, he would update the world. He projected all this on the screen so Cai and Sage could comment and help him with the language, ensuring it was compassionate enough.

When he was done, Cai said, 'So what are the next steps, leader?' She looked at Hudson slyly.

"Well, we wait for the results of the autopsy. They will exhume the body within the next week, and we should know if they found anything. I'm hoping they will announce it publicly to quiet down the uproar that's been building against them."

Chapter 27

As they waited for the autopsy results, time slowed down for the three friends. It turns out that life's daily mundane chores aren't as engaging when you could be doing something interesting and challenging, like solving crimes. Hudson, Cai, and Sage were all bored to tears by the rigid school structure and everything else as they waited for updates from the police department and the county coroner.

Hudson took the time further to solidify his online connections in the true crime sphere, ensuring he was in touch with all the major blogs and podcasts. After the Dylan case, he was now on people's radar, and with the 'Get Justice for Isabelle' case, he became a well-known name in similar digital circles. Hudson was building a significant following on his web pages and social media channels, which he set up to support the various causes they were investigating. His followers had gone from a few thousand to tens of thousands, and he was on the cusp of hundreds of thousands. Even watching murder shows while enjoying their daily after-school cereal wasn't as much fun as it used to be. After all, this real-life mystery had the kids themselves leading it, not the untouchable heroes seen on TV who always come to the rescue at just the right time.

In turn, to keep their interest piqued, the kids had gotten deeper into connected true crime stories. Recently, they had begun turning their attention to serial killers and watching a variety of short-run documentaries on legendary murderers like John Wayne Gacy and Ted Bundy. Hudson was fascinated by the psychological analysis of these deviants and saw integrating profiling into their investigations as a key step towards advancing their various cases.

He understood that to catch a sick mind, you needed to think like one. The deviant does not think or act like normal people, so you cannot apply rational logic to discern their behavior. Hudson thought that it only made sense that if serial killers had a certain way of thinking and behaving, then other criminals would have similar personality traits that they could use to slim down their POI list. From his reading, Hudson knew the FBI and various police departments had been doing behavioral profiling of high-level suspects since the 1970s.

Going forward, Hudson ensured each of the dossiers he put together for the team included a profiling page. The page would include a behavioral analysis, demographic information, and pictures to give the team a more rounded look at who they were targeting.

Finally, after about a week or two of waiting, Hudson updated the club on the autopsy status during the next Operation: Middle Finger check-in meeting. As soon as the news hit, he was informed by a local news story. He then amplified that announcement on his page and to his followers, who then shared it with a much wider audience of millions of people worldwide.

"The results are in!" Hudson was beaming. The girls could tell this was good news, at least for the investigation.

"The coroner did the autopsy, and Isabelle, as expected, had toxic levels of NoxyRotin still in her bone marrow, clearly showing she died from an overdose. The coroner has updated her CoD, that is, the Cause of Death, for you amateurs out there." Hudson got no reaction, as expected.

"And her death is no longer listed as 'natural causes' and has now been classified as 'accidental death from overdose.'

Cai and Sage were so excited that they jumped up and high-fived Hudson, who was just as excited, with a big smile on his face. After a few moments, Sage was the first to pull back her excitement a bit. She felt instinctively guilty for celebrating someone else's bad fortune.

"I'm glad we helped to expose this guy, but we should show some respect to the dead. This girl was killed, either through criminal negligence or incompetence. I guess I'm feeling a little ashamed for being so excited for our success at her expense."

Hudson and Cai got what Sage was saying. Both of them had learned a lot about empathy and, well, just being decent from Sage. They knew to default to her in these grayer areas of the human experience. They both respectfully pulled back their excitement a bit to be more reflective of the pain this poor child had been through.

"So, the cops now know how she died, but will they do anything about it?" Cai asked.

"Hmm, good question, Cai," Hudson was thinking. "Well, they are in deep now in a PR sense. They went and did the autopsy and announced it publicly, thinking they would find nothing and all this would go away. But they did find something, and now they are in a pickle. I can think of no other path but for them to investigate it further. Now, the parents will not file charges as they want to keep it quiet. But the cops have to pursue it. Interesting."

"We need to keep the pressure up, Hudson." Sage was getting it quickly. She had also learned from Hudson and Cai and had become more street-smart. "Sure, we won the battle here, but not the war. If things die down, the cops will bury this."

"Yep," Cai agreed. "And I think we need to start putting pressure on the parents. They need to feel the squeeze here so that they are the ones putting pressure on the cops to find out what happened to their kid. They must be publicly humiliated and shamed until they act like parents should be acting."

"I think you are right, Cai," Hudson replied. "At first, it made sense to put pressure on the cops only, but now we need the parents to step up. It's time to shine the light on them."

'So, what do we do?" Cai was thinking.

Sage jumped in before Hudson could: "What about another video from us? Update the Justice for Isabelle crowd online, get people worked up to share this video, and put pressure on the parents and police to finish this investigation."

"I like it," Hudson was thinking deeper, too. "This video is more about the results of the autopsy, and parents everywhere need to come together to get justice for Isabelle! We will shame her parents publicly for not supporting an inquiry and charges against the hospital and doctor. Who knows, we may be able to put some pressure on Lyzer about Noxy. Make them change their messaging or something."

Chapter 28

Their new video followed a format similar to their previous ones. The Cereal Club was quickly learning what worked to trigger people's emotions and get them to react. A similar lesson had been learned by media companies and the rich people who owned them centuries ago. In this instance, the kids wanted to generate shame and guilt from parents, which, as it turns out, is pretty easy.

Perhaps most parents aren't as on top of their game as they'd like others to think they are. Maybe these parents are hiding their culpability in the mismanagement of their children and feel tremendous guilt for doing so. So, when they see a child who has been mistreated, they react angrily and strongly, more so than healthy and well-meaning parents. It's an interesting psychological dichotomy that Hudson was prepared to exploit.

The video began with Hudson, Cai, and Sage in front of the hospital. There was a mist in the air and a somber tone to the proceedings. The kids were forlorn, their heads cast down, as the details of Isabelle and her fate flashed on the screen in a series of text blurbs and pictures to guide viewers. The kids took turns narrating the script Hudson had written.

"JUSTICE for Isabelle, NOW!" All three said in unison, choking back the tears.

The camera focused on Sage. "Isabelle overdosed on NoxyRotin. Why?"

It then moved to Cai, a tear glimmering in her tiny eye, "How many children around the country have died from NoxyRotin?"

Hudson then looked more sternly at the camera as it turned to him, "What are parents doing to protect their children from incompetent doctors misprescribing dangerous medications to them?"

Now it was Sage's turn again, looking much more critically at the camera, "Doesn't Lyzer care about children's health? Shouldn't they do more to warn parents and doctors about the danger of Noxy?"

The camera then zooms in slightly on Cai. She didn't mince words, "There must be justice for Isabelle, now! How can parents put their careers and their company's profits ahead of their daughter's safety? How can such people not seek justice for their daughter?"

The camera then zoomed out to include all three speakers. "JUSTICE for Isabell, NOW!" they said, as it was splashed across the screen in large font. During the fadeout, a list of website URLs, email addresses, social media pages, and other contact information was displayed to encourage sharing and following.

The results were explosive. Hudson had already built up a significant online following, while Sage was very popular at school and had a pretty sizable following, too. They were starting with a good base to begin amplifying their messaging, and with an appropriately emotionally manipulative video, it hit the sweet spot and went viral. Within 24 hours, they had 3.5 million views and tens of thousands of new followers on all of Hudson's channels and pages, now a small network of interconnected pages supporting each other.

After a few more days of public outrage across the worldwide internet, the wheels started turning at the hospital, at Lyzer, and at the police. Angry parents have a way of making themselves heard. They took to their phones, the internet, and text apps to express their feelings about the doctor, the medication, the company that made it, and the parents who chose not to hold these people accountable. The snowball was rolling, and things were not looking good for the accused.

The hospital was the first one to make an announcement. The doctor who performed the procedure and gave Isabelle the dose of NoxyRotin that killed her was suspended from his position without pay, pending a full investigation. The hospital made a public apology for the death of the child and promised to work with the investigators to get to the bottom of the situation.

Next, the Lyzer marketing and PR teams got together to review the case and plan their response. They immediately issued a statement stating that doctors should not prescribe NoxyRotin to children under eighteen years old under any circumstances. They further noted that this was always their guidance and that they were reiterating it. Lyzer PR also reminded the public that Noxy had been emergency-approved by the FDA, and the FDA said it was safe, so there was nothing to worry about.

Finally, Isabel's parents, Bob and Karen, made their first and only public appearance in a local news clip, expressing their dismay over everything that had happened. They told the interviewer they had no idea their company manufactured the drug that killed their child and that they were in the dark here as much as anyone else. Bob and Karen told the cameras they fully supported an investigation and would do anything they could to help the police investigate the case and ensure the responsible parties are held accountable.

Then, the Old Springs Community Police Department made a brief printed statement. They said the case was now an active criminal case and would be investigated until it was resolved.

It took months and months for the case to be fully resolved. What was incontrovertible was the fact that the doctor who did the procedure misprescribed NoxyRotin to a twelve-year-old child and was criminally negligent for doing so. Like most cases in the US, they rarely go to trial as the prosecutors work to bully defendants into accepting plea deals to keep the cases out of the courts. The doctor was fired from his job, lost his medical license, and received a conviction for negligent homicide. He was sentenced to seven years in a minimum-security country club prison and was released in three years on parole.

Within a few months, Bob and Karen lost their jobs at Lyzer. It turns out companies don't like bad PR any more than the cops do, and this couple who sacrificed justice for their child to advance their corporate careers were thrown to the curb by the very same company. Neither were given severance packages and were blackballed from the pharmaceutical industry for the rest of their lives. Bob eventually tried to open his own bagel shop, which failed within the first year. Karen tried her hand at a scented candle business, but that only cost them more money than they made. Eventually, Bob and Karen divorced and lived in single-bedroom apartments on opposite sides of town. Forever alone, their careers and positions no longer supported them or gave them an identity. Without their corporate personas to define them and provide them with purpose, they were shells of their former selves and faded into the dreary wallpaper of everyday life.

Chapter 29

The changes in both Hudson's and Sage's lives due to their successful investigations into child abuse and negligence were significant, to say the least. Hudson had never had any friends before, IRL or online, and the fact that he now had two real friends, thousands of online connections, and millions of followers totally changed the tone and complexity of his life. He used to spend most days in self-imposed isolation, playing his games, watching his programs, and focusing on his hobbies and interests. Now, there was a constant storm of activity and outreach to Hudson, mostly from his online community, seeking his assistance in amplifying their issues and supporting their causes. Hudson was only too happy to assist if the cause was authentic and the victims deserved it.

For Sage, her popularity at school blew through the roof, and she was now the 'It' girl in the school district. She was already pretty, with a hip look and attitude, and it was easy for the in-crew of jocks, cute girls, and popular kids to let her into their circles. Sage was fun and had a positive attitude toward life, so people were naturally drawn to her. The fact that she was indigenous didn't seem to matter too much, as she was mixed race with some European in there, so her facial features would not assault the delicate ego of the predominating white Anglo-Saxon students.

Sadly, for Cai, she saw little to no benefit from their success, unlike her two friends. She was too black to be accepted by the white students, and there just weren't any black students in the school for her to associate with. She was simply the only one, and she stood out like a sore thumb. Cai was the school's token black student and was the focus of all their infantile racist rage passed down from each student's bigoted parents. There would be no easy way out of this maze for Cai.

While their personal lives were growing and changing in myriad ways, Operation: Middle Finger was languishing. Sure, they had been eliminating POIs instead of turning them into suspects, which was a primary goal of any investigation. And it's not like they were not doing good things or making progress. Their investigation had helped turn them into child rights advocates, helping to provide a voice to forgotten children who have no adult looking out for them. It turns out there are millions of kids out there who are being used and abused by some nefarious adult, many times their very own parents or guardians. You know, the people who are supposed to be protecting children.

The club had one more set of very promising POIs, but they all felt like they needed to refocus the investigation. Were they on the right track here? Was a crime actually committed against whoever lost that finger? If so, what was the crime? Since they started the investigation months ago, the kids were no closer to finding out who that little finger belonged to.

During one of their heated discussions on what direction they should take, Sage reminded Hudson and Cai that her father, a Shuar shaman, was willing to do a vision quest to try to find out who the finger belonged to. In fact, he was already preparing for the journey. Hudson tried to be open-minded, but anything spiritual or mystic made him uncomfortable. He just didn't 'get it.'

"I think it's a good idea, Sage, but I'm not sure there is anything I can contribute to there. It's just really far out from what I know." Hudson was trying to be empathetic.

"I hear you, Hudson." Sage was very understanding and not pushy at all. "No one is trying to get you to be uncomfortable or do something you don't believe in. But I will tell you that you don't need to participate; just watch and absorb. If you can tolerate a few hours of minor physical discomfort, you may find it beneficial as it can support our traditional investigative techniques."

Hudson was intrigued. Sage explained it to him exactly how he needed to hear it, without pressure, shame, or condescension. He knew he needed to do more behavioral analysis of his suspects; maybe this was a way to get closer to them and understand their motivations and behaviors.

Hudson looked at Cai. "Are you going to be there?" He had come to see Cai as his protector, and having her around made him more comfortable overall.

"Yeah, sure, Hud. I have nothing better to do anyway." Cai was smiling reassuringly.

"Great!" Sage was visibly excited. "I'll set up a time with my father and let you guys know when and where to show up. Trust me, you both will find this really interesting and enlightening. Just keep an open mind, OK?"

Chapter 30

The wind was howling through the trees as Hudson and Cai followed Sage deep into the woods behind Sage's home. Hudson had never been out in the woods at night, and it turns out it was scary as hell. There were weird shadows everywhere as the moon shone through the branches, and the wind moved them in strange and unnatural ways.

In front of them and leading the way were a handful of Shuar tribesmen and women, including Sage's father, the shaman, known as uwishin. As they walked through the woods, Sage quietly instructed them on how to behave, what to expect, and what the ceremony was about.

"First off, guys, being quiet and respectful is important. I know you guys would be, but I'm just making sure. Shuar takes this process and their beliefs very seriously. If we disrupt or taint the proceedings in any way, we can undermine their ability to envision a solution to our problem.

"For Shuar, we believe that our uwishin have tremendous power and can talk to the spirits of the natural world. They can commune with nature and harness the energy of the plants and animals around them. To tap into this power and harness it, the uwishin will oversee a ritual that includes chanting, drumming, and dancing, and they will ingest a sacred plant to guide them on their journey.

"My father has spent days preparing natem, a jungle vine from our homeland. This is the main ingredient to prepare ayahuasca, a mind-altering religious sacrament that will allow the participants to enter a vision journey.

"This process can be very dangerous, so no children are permitted to do it, which is one reason why they have agreed to assist us. People's visions during this journey are considered prophetic, so this is no joke, and a fun time trip like US college students have. These visions are real and tell us about the past, the present, and the future. Visions can be positive or negative, depending on what the travelers try to do during the trip. Positive visions are called kuntukar, and negative visions are called mesekramprar." Sage had a feeling this night would be leaning towards the latter.

"Now, there is a deeper experience that few Shuar can venture into. This is typically reserved for experienced uwishin. It's called penke karamprar, and that is when a traveler visits the spirit of a dead relative or friend. I am not sure this can be done with someone the uwishin does not know personally, but I believe my father will attempt this.

Both Hudson and Cai kept their mouths shut as Sage was talking. Hudson was scared shitless of the dark woods and did his best to focus on what she was saying. Cai was intimidated, too, but she was so used to being tough that she didn't let it show. She kept a straight face and decided to follow instructions and keep her mouth shut. But this was plain weird and out there as far as she was concerned.

After about twenty minutes of walking, which felt like two hours to Hudson, they approached a clearing in the woods. There were logs on their side, arranged in a circle that had been flattened so you could sit on them. There were also posts arranged in a circle that the Shuar hung their lanterns on to illuminate the clearing. With the lanterns, the moonlight, the wind, and the moving trees and branches, the clearing took on a spectral quality that was unsettling and intriguing at once. Sage led Hudson and Cai to the farthest log from the group, setting the kids on the outer fringe of the prayer circle.

"Guys, we will sit here and observe. We are part of the ceremony by being present, but we are not active members. But our thoughts and feelings matter in this process and can affect the visions and journeys of the different participants. So, we must keep our minds clear and try not to let events or what people are going through affect or frighten us too much. We need to be open-minded, not judgmental and critical."

Hudson and Cai nodded and followed instructions, but both were a little intimidated by what Sage had just said.

"Frightened how?" Hudson didn't want to sound scared, but he was.

"Well," Sage looked at Hudson very compassionately, "these participants, and my father, will ingest a mystical substance and engage in rituals that may be shocking to witness for a newbie. You need not worry or get frightened by their behavior or what you see. This is a millennia-old ceremony managed by a shaman with years of experience. Put your trust in him and his ability to control and oversee this vision journey."

Hudson and Cai promised to do their best. Hudson just wanted this to be over as soon as possible. All he wanted was to be back in the safety of his own bedroom, with his computers, music, and everything else that mattered. He decided he would never go back into the woods at night again if he could help it. He was happy he was forward-thinking enough to pack a backpack with water, drinks, snacks, his phone, and everything else he needed to soothe him during this stressful experience.

All the Shuar were dressed in traditional clothing made and designed specifically for the ritual they were about to undergo. The clothing was considered sacred, hand-made and hand-dyed, with beautiful, intricate patterns and designs that held deep, eternal meaning for the Shuar and their spirit ancestors. On their ears, they wore feather ornaments called akitiai, which were made of toucan feathers, beetle wing covers, and glass beads.

Karakras, the shaman, or uwishin, began the ceremony by unveiling the sacred symbols and artifacts that would guide them through their spiritual journey. First, he took out his traditional bag woven from chambira leaves. The bag, like their traditional clothes, was adorned with intricate designs and patterns that could only be discerned by Shuar with a deep understanding of their people and history. Karakras held up the bag to show everyone what held all his tools and offerings. Upon opening the bag, Karakras took out the tumi, a ceremonial knife that represented the uwishins' power and ability to protect.

Under her breath, Sage explained the items to Hudson and Cai, "That knife contains its own energy, and it is believed the uwishin can ward off evil spirits during the ceremony with it." Hudson shivered a bit.

Also taken from the bag was the pre-prepared ayahuasca mixture in a traditional Shuar sacred cup, ready for the various travelers to consume. After taking all the items from the bag and showing them to the participants, the group began chanting and playing quena flute melodies, supported by traditional Shuar instruments, to commune with nature and the spirits. One Shuar took out a small drum and provided a beat and a sense of time to their chant and flute playing.

Then Karakras began to give ayahuasca to each of the travelers through the sacred cup, himself being the last. Each ingested it to the rhythm of the drums, the melody of the flutes, and the drone of their chants. The mixture made each traveler retch with an awful, bitter taste and smell.

"The travelers will continue to chant and play until the sacred medicine kicks in. They will all get violently ill from it, throwing up and getting sick. It is considered the price for commuting with the spirits and nature, and is a cleansing process for them."

Hudson did not like this at all. Now, people were going to get physically ill in front of him? Was Sage kidding him with this stuff?

Sage continued her narration, "The Shuar believe that everything in the natural world—plants, animals, whatever it is—has a spirit within it. Everything has a spirit that can be communicated with by the shaman and the travelers they guide through their spirit journeys. Travelers can connect with spirits to better understand their lives or the world, ask for protection from evil spirits or bad people, or help create a sense of well-being in their community.

"The chants are critical to enabling their journey. They have meaning that goes back thousands of years and are sacred, helping guide participants on their trip. It will take a little time as the visionary medicine kicks in, and they will begin their journeys.

"From our perspective, we will not know exactly what they experienced until after the shaman communes with the travelers, interprets their experiences, and communicates to us, hopefully, the information we are looking for. We may find out more or less than we wanted to know. It all depends on what the spirits want to communicate to us."

For the next several hours, the kids watched the participants get sicker and sicker, vomiting and having uncontrollable diarrhea. It was not a pleasant sight, and Hudson made sure not to watch anything that made him feel sick. After the initial phases, the participants began to feel the effects of the sacred medicine, and each started their own journey, all within their own heads and personal experiences. The travelers talked to people the kids could not see and had revelations far beyond the average person's understanding. Some of their actions and words were nonsense, while some seemed to have some esoteric meaning that would make sense if only the kids could see what the traveler was seeing. They would have to wait for Karakras, the uwishin, to tell them what he had learned from his travelers and what he saw and experienced himself.

Chapter 31

Karakras had been on dozens of spirit journeys before, and he had been uwishin to guide others in their journeys at least a hundred times. While there was nothing totally new to him in this process, the experience was always different, always unique, and always distinct. The spirits he talked to, the insights he received, and the visions he had could never be predicted. You may want an answer or insight into one area, only to receive something completely different. But this night would be different, as he was attempting a vision and journey he had never taken before.

On a few occasions, Karakras performed penke karamprar, a ritual journey in which the traveler speaks directly to a deceased relative or friend. He had done this to commune with his great ancestors and alleviate the pain of a saddened widow or mother, but he had never attempted to perform this ritual to communicate with an unknown person.

He brought the finger of the missing child with him, feeling that this finger must still contain the person's spirit, which he can connect with. If this were the case, he thought he had a chance to uncover a hidden truth and secure justice for this poor child. If not, he could be putting himself at significant risk for a poor mesekramprar, or what US kids in the 60s would call a 'bad trip.' Karakras knew that all great knowledge was acquired with some risk, and, as an experienced uwishin, he believed he could take the risk in this situation.

Once the ayahuasca began to kick in, Karakras knew this was going to be a vision like no other. The potion felt stronger and more potent than ever before, even though he prepared it in the same fashion as he always had. He knew that strong spirits were at work, guiding the creation of the sacred medicine, and that they had ensured it was strong enough for him to go on the journey he needed. They must have guided his hands during the creation in ways he was unaware of.

He knew his first step was to release his ego and his desire for control, and to give in to the all-encompassing, interconnected universe. To do this, he performed a simple meditation visualization during the ritual. He imagined himself floating down a river. He knew, as he floated, that he could only follow the river in the direction it moved. He had to give in to the river's current and not fight against it too much. Yes, he could move a little to avoid a disaster while he floated, but going against the river's flow was a life of struggle and futility.

He remembered a song he liked, by Bob Dylan, if he was correct, and it said, "The river flows, it flows to the sea, and wherever that river flows, that's where I want to be." Karakras smiled at the song, which somehow fit with the ancient chants and the melodic music played by the Shuar in the background. All things are one. All things flow from one. All things connect to one. He prayed and chanted, waiting for the spirits to speak and guide him through his journey.

Suddenly, the known world disappeared from Karakras' vision; the trees and dancing shadows blended, and the light around him began to pulse to what seemed like the beat of his heart. Or was it the heart of the forest and the world around him? Colors burst into his vision in the dark, dreary woods, exploding into a kaleidoscopic feast. Karakras was then thrust into a tunnel of bright light with geometric patterns and an intricate lattice of mathematical details expressed in points and waves of light and being.

His essence, who Karakras was as a person, melded with the environment and merged with nature, as his inner being and true self emerged, dispensing the mask he was required to wear in the known world. His old self was gone now, and all that was tangible disappeared. He was part of a deeper and broader universe that most people will never be able to interact with.

Now nothing more than a particle of light, or a collection of particles, the traveler being that was once Karakras moved as fast as the speed of light, being light himself, and merged fully into the one all-encompassing universe. There was no more distinction between himself and nature, between him and animal, between him and plant. They were all one, all from the same source, all with the same essence. The being known as Karakras now has no weight, dimension, or space in time. He is the universe, and the universe is he.

Within this mass of light and matter, within this ever-expanding and ever-contracting universe, while traveling at the speed of light and not moving at all, the being once known as Karakras encountered the Sentinel, a spirit being of immense power and eternal love. This being had form, unlike the being once known as Karakras, and its form looked humanoid but was definitely not human. While it had form, it was also somewhat formless and semi-lucent. The being once known as Karakras knew instinctively that this being could take any form or be without corporeal shape, as it wished it, so it was. The being was not just part of the universe but the universe itself, as were all things for all time, immortal. No beginning, no end, all within the great wheel of time and space, forever growing and dying, repeated endlessly.

The Sentinel spoke to the traveler, but the spirit guide did not use words in the traditional sense. The traveler did not see the Sentinel's mouth move if it indeed had a mouth.

Instead, the being once known as Karakras heard the Sentinel directly in his mind, or what was once his mind, which now was just a part of the more expansive universe, which was probably why they could communicate in such a way.

When the Sentinel spoke, they spoke of all things at once, through all time in past, present, and future, and all of space, in all dimensions, and all points of light. Even with the full weight of the universe integrated into him, the being once known as Karakras had trouble discerning what the spirit guide was trying to communicate to him. Almost like a shotgun blast of information to his head, he had to pick out a few pellets coming at him at light speed, stop them with his mind, disassemble them, and analyze them with all the power of his now universally integrated mind head.

But which ones should Karakras focus on? All of it was so wonderful and frightening at the same time. There were so many questions, so many secrets, and so much time to discover them. He wanted to stay in this state of non-decision forever, in the light and warming love-glow of the Sentinel, with infinite possibilities and pathways open to his spirit, never taking any one path and never limiting himself to any single doctrine. The being once known as Karakras almost lost himself in this fantasy, between a world of possibility and dream.

But the traveler knew he had a purpose. He did not know what that purpose was or why a spirit being like himself would care about the goings-on in the corporeal world. Their concerns seemed so trivial to the universe overall. Small and insignificant issues that come and go in the space of a millisecond in the eternity of time immortal were the concerns of plants and animals unconnected to the spirit world.

The spirit being, once known as Karakras, had enough memory left to realize he had not always been a spirit being and might not always be in this state of infinite ecstasy, and that he was, in fact, here for a reason that mattered to others he cared about. He tried to reimagine his corporeal body, what it looked like in the circle in the woods, and the things he had with him. He remembered the fire, the circle, the chanting, and the music. It was all so beautiful and strange. He reached down and saw he had a bag with various items inside. He reached into the bag and took out a small object. It was very odd to him, this little thing. What was it? It looked like a stick or a large worm. But it was hard and had a bone, not like a worm, which was soft and squishy. He then realized it was not an animal or plant but part of an animal. Ah, now he knew what he was looking at. It was a small finger, probably from a human child. And with that realization, the finger began to hum and vibrate, catching the Sentinel's notice. The Sentinel reached down to touch the finger. When it did, the finger split open, and a kaleidoscope of colors and geometric shapes exploded from it, opening another tunnel of light that the being once known as Karakras fell into.

Chapter 32

The next day, Hudson, Cai, and Sage met for their daily weekday cereal and to digest the previous night's events. Hudson was still recovering from the experience. During it, he was cold, frightened, hungry, thirsty, and creeped out by all the strange rituals, chants, and drugged-out behavior of the spirit travelers. It was unlike anything he had ever seen, and he was still uneasy about it the next day. Cai had a similar reaction, but she was made of sterner stuff, so she kept her mouth shut as she absorbed what were, to her, very odd behaviors. She was, in a way, more open-minded than Hudson about cultural issues.

Sage was somewhat surprised by both her friends' queasiness. Here were a couple of self-proclaimed tough guys who were fine with dismembered fingers but were all namby-pamby when it came to a simple Indigenous ritual. She would have to think about this contradiction and reflect on it. The fear of the unknown, the unknowable, is a powerful motivator or a demotivator, depending on how one looks at it.

"Sage, do you want to take the lead on the summary from last night?" Hudson asked sheepishly. He was tired and stressed, and didn't have much energy to put on a happy face. He didn't know why it bothered people so much when he didn't always act happy, but apparently, it did. If he ever told the truth to people when they asked how he was feeling, they got noticeably upset with him, so he didn't bother anymore. Why did they ask if they didn't really want to know?

"Sure, Hudson." Sage felt the exact opposite of Hudson. Last night's ritual reinvigorated her; the sights, sounds, and mystery of the event were exciting and enticing. It made her feel more connected to her family, people, and culture, something that Hudson couldn't understand, being a community of one.

"Well, first, thank you both for coming to the ritual and being so respectful and patient. I am sure from your perspectives it was pretty weird and out there, but if someone from another world came and saw your rituals around Christmas and Thanksgiving, they may find them just as bizarre."

Sage felt good about finally getting her time in the spotlight. She hoped she would be able to bring some more dynamic understanding of the broader world to her friends, respectfully and considerately.

"Now, it will take a little time for my father to confer with the other travelers. He will meditate on what they told him and his own experience, so he can communicate it to us so we can comprehend it." Sage's eyes were sparkling. She was incredibly proud of her father and how strong and brave he was to experience such ground-shaking events. "But I can tell you he communed with me at home after the ritual and said he had a profound experience that taught him much about our particular mystery. He took the finger with him into the spirit realm and communed with an ancient spirit known as the Sentinel, who communicated something about it to him."

Hudson and Cai were on the edge of their seats, excited. Sage looked totally serious about what she was saying, so they took everything she said at face value.

"As I said, my father will meditate on it and tell me his insights shortly, but I am very confident that the universe will point us in the right direction. We must be patient and proceed with our investigation; everything will come to pass as it should." Sage seemed so confident in the validity of her culture's process that Hudson and Cai felt satisfied as well. They knew their good friend would never lead them astray, and they just needed to trust her.

"Thank you, Sage." Hudson was very appreciative not to have to take the lead on this portion of the investigation. It was disquieting to him, frankly. He was much more confident dealing with data, processes, facts, and traditional problem-solving.

"While we wait for feedback from Sage's father, let's look at our final primary POI. If this lead doesn't turn anything up, I think it makes sense to discuss next steps and whether we should pursue Operation: Middle Finger indefinitely."

Cai was nodding in agreement. "That makes sense, Hud. We can't keep spinning our wheels forever. I mean, this operation has led to multiple successful, non-related operations in uncovering child neglect and abuse. But we haven't really made much progress on determining who this finger belonged to or if there was a crime committed."

The reality was that none of them wanted to give up. This after-school hobby quickly became their main activity, occupying most of their waking thoughts and sometimes their dreams. This was far more enticing and exciting than school or any mundane chore a kid does during their typical day. They were making things happen, good things, and it was clear to the kids that if they didn't do it, no adult would bother.

"I hear you, Cai. But I have a good feeling about our next POI. For the first time, we are going to look at an adult who is not wealthy. This one is a small-business owner and is younger than the others. His name is Nico, and he owns the tattoo and CBD shop we pass on the way to school.

"Now, this guy filed a police report for a missing child a few years ago. While I was able to find information on the missing child report, I couldn't find any information on the child's recovery or updates on the case. So, it feels like there is something up here. Why was more fuss not made over this kid when they went missing? It begs for us to look into it a bit more."

"Yeah, but how, Hud?" Cai was thinking, but not coming up with anything good. "This is an adult business. I don't think anyone under 18 can get a tattoo legally, so any of us hanging around that shop asking a lot of dumb questions will be noticed big time."

"Good points, Cai," Hudson said, wiping his glasses for the hundredth time today. "We just need an excuse to get in there and poke around. You know, ask a few questions, see what we see. If we don't get anything upfront, we take it on the sly and poke into their mail or electronic communications." Hudson was smirking. "That is only a last resort if the ends justify the means."

Sage liked that better. Deliberately invading innocent people's privacy was not something she was OK with. But, if they were murderers, then she thought it was all right to spy if it got them closer to bringing that person to justice. If the cops would actually do their job, then the Cereal Club wouldn't have to. But since they didn't, it was up to the kids to do what was right, even if it meant bending the rules. The team took a few minutes to reflect, eating snacks and sipping juice. After a few minutes, Hudson jumped out of his seat.

"I got it!" He exclaimed. "I know somebody who has always wanted a tattoo; maybe with a little convincing and me offering to pay for it, he would be interested in helping us out."

"Who?" Cai was intrigued.

"My lovely brother Brody, of course."

Chapter 33

Hudson knew that approaching Brody directly and asking for help would lead nowhere. He could envision no conversation in which Brody did not laugh at him and dismiss him outright. Hudson would have to find another way. He knew that for someone like Brody, a young man wrapped up in himself and his wants and needs, appealing to his vanity and ego was the way to go.

Hudson began by slipping comments into casual conversation about how cool he thought tattoos were while they were watching TV or a movie. While watching a streaming version of the old John Carpenter movie 'Escape from New York', Hudson noticed that the main character's name was 'Snake' and that he had a big cobra tattoo on his chest.

"Damn, that is so badass!" Hudson was saying, pretending not to notice Brody in the room. "Someday, I am going to get a big snake tattoo on my chest, and I want people to call me 'Snake!'"

"Give me a break," Brody was laughing at Hudson. "You wouldn't last two minutes under the needle. That hurts like hell."

"How would you know?" Hudson was challenging him directly. "It's not like you ever got a tattoo."

Brody stopped smiling. "Listen, you little punk. If I wanted a tattoo, I would get one; it's just that simple."

"You wish." Hudson was not going to back down this time. "First off, you need to be eighteen. You are not old enough. Besides, Dad would kill you. You'd have to get it on your butt or something!" Hudson started laughing.

Brody got up from his chair and moved in on Hudson, getting in his face and physically intimidating him.

"Watch it, ass wipe. For your information, I have been planning on getting a tattoo. I don't need to wait until I'm eighteen, and I don't need Dad's permission, either."

'Ok, ok,' Hudson knew when to back off. "What are you thinking of getting?"

"I don't know exactly, something freaking cool. Something the chicks will like."

"If you want me to help you pick something out, I can go down with you. I promise I won't tell Dad anything."

Brody thought about it for a minute. It wouldn't be a bad idea to get a different opinion, so he didn't pick something dumb. He could always go down, take a look around, and get one later.

"Sure, why the hell not? Let's go down and see what they got."

They passed it daily, but neither had been in The Inner Mind Tattoo and CBD Parlor. It was one of those places for adults that kids don't even think about going into, like a paint store. Well, until they get into their mid-to-late teens and want to impress the girls or boys. Then they start to think about being cool and all the stupid stuff that goes along with being so self-conscious. Hudson liked being fourteen just fine; he liked his female friends but never thought about getting a tattoo for one of them. Who knows why it was so easy to push Brody over the edge to get one, but the fact that he already wanted one made it easier.

Once at the front door, Hudson waited for Brody to go in first. Brody was hesitant, though, as he looked both ways to ensure no adults or police were in sight. Once Brody saw that Hudson was not going in before him, he went in, and Hudson slipped in behind him. Inside, it was dim, like twilight, even though it was midday. There were lots of cool things on the walls, like comic book art, and lots of creepy things, like skulls, masks, and kitschy types of things twenty- and thirty-something hipsters seem to love having around.

Hudson scanned the room and noticed what looked like an authentic monkey skull adorned with beads and feathers. He also saw what looked like voodoo dolls, Hindu and Buddhist statues, and other oddities he didn't know much about. Hudson found it all fascinating, but after being at an actual Indigenous ritual not a few days prior, he knew this was a cheap facsimile of what was authentic for people like the Shuar. He knew that no one from this culture could understand or take the intimate and ancient practices from another culture seriously, so foreign to them that they may as well be from another universe.

In addition to all this visual feast, there was a large, burly, long-bearded man inside. He was covered in tattoos, wearing sunglasses, and looked just as scary and intimidating as he probably wanted people to think he was. He was behind the counter, and once he saw the two kids walk in, his demeanor did not improve.

"What do you guys want? This place is for adults eighteen or older." After the first glance, he barely looked at the kids, as if they were wasting his valuable time. This reminded Hudson of the way the police talked to them when they brought them the finger.

Brody spoke up first. "Sorry to bother you, sir. I was looking to get a tattoo—my first, actually." Brody was deferring to the store owner and hoping to get some compassion from him.

It worked a bit. The tattoo store owner softened his attitude, looked Brody up and down, and said, "Ah, looking to get your first tattoo, huh? You're a little young, no? How old are you?"

Brody knew he would have to show ID, so he didn't bother lying, "I'm sixteen, sir. I didn't know there was an age limit."

That only made the story owner smile a bit more. He paused for a few seconds, looked at Hudson, then back at Brody, shaking his head.

"I'm sorry, son, but you must be eighteen and have an ID to prove it. Otherwise, I can lose my license."

Brody and Hudson didn't know what else to say, so they turned around and started walking out the door. Hudson went first, and as Brody was walking out, the store owner gestured to him to come back in, alone. Brody told Hudson to wait on the front step while he stepped back into the store.

The store owner whispered to Brody, making sure Hudson could not hear. "Listen, kid. I'm not one to stand in the way of a young man wanting to get his first tattoo. If you are interested, I may be able to procure you a fake ID that says you are eighteen so you can get this legally."

Brody was intrigued, to say the least. If he got a fake ID, it could be used for all sorts of things beyond just getting the tattoo. "How much are we talking about?"

The owner smiled; he knew he had a fish on the line. "Well, it depends on what you want. I can get you anything from a basic driver's license ID for about $120 to more serious identification like a passport or Real ID. But then we get into money, like $1000 or more. Hell, I can even get you a whole new identity if you want."

The owner then backed off a bit. He had gotten a little too excited and maybe revealed more than he should have. This kid would never go for those high-end products, and there was no reason to expose himself too much here. Ah, who cares, he thought. Who was this kid going to tell anyway?

Chapter 34

It didn't take much for Hudson to convince Brody to return and get the fake ID and tattoo. Even Hudson was excited that Brody could get them things they usually couldn't, like renting a car. Brody figured he was about one hundred dollars short, depending on the kind of tattoo he wanted, and Hudson had promised to loan him the rest. Hudson's little online t-shirt business was doing pretty well, and it afforded him a few bucks to grease the wheels in situations like this.

Brody didn't want to bring Hudson, but Hudson made it clear that the condition of the loan was that he watch the tattoo procedure. Brody said it was fine, but he told Hudson to wait outside while he negotiated for the fake ID and then come inside. This way, the owner would feel more comfortable and probably not push back on Hudson watching the tattooing.

They went in when they thought it would not be busy, in the middle of a weekday, a little after lunchtime. It was easy for Hudson to sneak out of school for a few minutes at a time; no one really noticed when he was around or not. Once there, Brody went inside while Hudson waited on the steps, and they completed the transaction for the fake driver's license. It was a quick deal, and as they were about to start picking a tattoo, Brody asked if his brother could come in to watch. The owner agreed.

Brody had picked out an American Traditional tattoo. He wanted to look badass, and those old-school tattoos like the ones sailors used to wear back in the day were coming back into style. He saw Traditionals like eagles, skulls, roses, daggers, and hearts. He was sold when he saw one with a heart and "Mom" written across the front. He pointed at that, and Hudson was pleasantly surprised. He didn't know Brody missed their mother like he did. Maybe Brody wasn't as much a shallow meathead as he had always thought him to be. Hudson would have to reflect on this a little more; perhaps, with people, there's more than meets the eye, and he shouldn't be too quick to judge what is on the surface by looks and attitude.

The owner, who introduced himself as Nico, seemed pleased with the choice. He commented that American Traditional were 'real' tattoos for 'real' people, and that 'New School cartoon stuff' was 'crap' and 'screw that' and on and on. Brody and Hudson nodded and agreed, not knowing what this guy was talking about.

Once the needle went into Brody's upper arm for the first time, he almost jumped out of the seat. He did not expect just how painful and uncomfortable getting a tattoo would be. It was not a pleasant affair. Hudson suppressed a laugh and the desire to mock his brother, as he felt differently about Brody now that he had decided to honor their mother. He felt closer to Brody, a little more protective of him.

Within a few minutes, Hudson could see that the owner, Nico, was completely engrossed in his current job, and Brody was so overwhelmed by pain that he was clenching his teeth and closing his eyes. Hudson took the opportunity to scan the room and noticed a set of beads blocking a door leading into the back room. He then started walking around the room, pretending to look at the stuff on the walls, while he edged closer and closer to the backroom. He gave it about fifteen minutes. Once he saw that both Nico and Brody were talking and deeply immersed in the tattooing process, Hudson slipped into the backroom.

Immediately, Hudson noticed this was not just a tattoo shop but a pretty extensive and sophisticated fake ID operation. He saw a computer, what looked like a laminating machine, and templates and samples of various in-state and out-of-state IDs. Some were in progress, and others looked like they were waiting for final touches. He snapped some pictures and videos to document the room's contents. There were lots of other documents and technologies he didn't quite understand, so he took pictures of them all, including close-ups of various items he found. There would be time to review all of this later with the whole crew. Within just a few minutes, Hudson was done and slipped back out, with both Brody and Nico never noticing that he was missing.

Soon, Brody's tattoo was done, and Hudson had to admit, it looked pretty cool. He has a tough, old-school Mom heart tattoo on his upper right arm. Pretty damn cool, Hudson thought. Brody was beyond excited, and the two of them walked home and talked like two friends, partners in crime, if you will, in a way they had never done before.

Chapter 35

The next day, Hudson and the team met for after-school cereal and to review the information from his outing with Brody. He hooked up his phone to the digital projector so they could review the pictures together and plan their next steps.

"On the surface, this looks like a standard fake ID operation." Hudson was back in his element, in control and presenting information to others. His adventure with Brody had re-energized him. It allowed him to connect with his brother in a way he never had before. He felt larger, more competent, and more whole.

"Nico is an alt hipster-type making a few bucks on the side doing IDs for kids who want to drink. No big deal, right? But then I started looking at these images in more detail. Take a look at this one." Hudson projected a picture of a birth certificate that was in the process of being modified.

"I don't get it. Why would they be making counterfeit birth certificates?" Sage asked. "What does someone do with that?"

"Great question, Sage. I did some research on it. One way to get higher-end fake IDs, which use modern technology as protection, is to use fake credentials to submit to authorities to get the actual documents." Hudson could tell they didn't get it. "Think of it like this. You go out and find a real person who is now dead, like someone who died when they were a kid. You make a fake birth certificate using their name and then use that along with an easy-to-make fake driver's license to assume the identity of that dead person.

Now, with those two documents, you can get real documents that are completely legit, like a passport."

Cai spoke up, "That seems pretty serious, Hud. How do they find out that information about kids who died? I mean, that's pretty hard to get, no?"

"I think you are right," Hudson said, agreeing. "They must have a partner or partners somewhere that are getting them that information so they can create these higher-end fake IDs. They need access to children's birth certificates, ones who died early, preferably, so no one else will be using that identity."

"So, we are talking about perhaps a government agency, or the high school, or hospital, maybe," Sage thought aloud. "They would have that kind of information if they knew someone who worked on the inside.

'Very insightful, Sage," Hudson was beaming. He had one more surprise that he had not shared yet. "Now check out this picture."

Hudson displayed the final picture of a folder with a birth certificate nearly done. The photo included supporting materials to enhance the document's legitimacy, including a fingerprint in ink on a small piece of paper. The fingerprint was nice and small, just like a young child's.

Both Sage and Cai almost fell out of their seats. Finally, after all this time, they were hopefully getting to the bottom of their mystery. It was the first hard lead they had gained, quickly turning tattoo shop owner Nico from POI into a suspect. Hudson was rolling now.

"Look, team, here is a guy creating fake IDs. Really high-end and expensive fake IDs. And as part of that process, he has a way of acquiring a child's fingerprint to support that documentation. And we just happened to find a severed child's finger. This may be the missing link we are looking for."

In Cai's brain, the tumblers were moving and clicking into place. She got it now. How could she not have seen it before? "I can only think of one place where someone is going to get a child's finger," Cai said, with her head down, as it was an unpleasant memory for her, "and that is the Old Springs Community Hospital Morgue."

Chapter 36

After the spirit journey, the Shuar uwishin Karakras spent some days conferring with the other travelers to interpret their experiences and reflect on his own experience. He had a vision like no other, and it took him some time to comprehend it so he could communicate its wisdom to his daughter and her friends. He knew right away from the vision that this was a far more complex situation than any of them had realized.

Karakras had never performed the penke karamprar on an unknown person before. It was a ritual typically reserved for communing with the spirits of loved ones, deceased friends, or long-dead relatives from ancient bloodlines. When he brought the finger to the Sentinel, an eternal being of unimaginable scope, it showed him the path to understanding.

There were deep and intimate links between the human psyche and the natural world. And as the natural world can be healthy or sick, in balance or out of balance, be growing or in decline, so can a human being. A person without a foundation of love and compassion, without a cohesive and rational structure to fall back on, can descend into the nether world of psychological misalignment, in which their ability to take in information and interact with the world at large is distorted by their inability to interpret things through a clear and accurate lens.

These distorted people are not what they seem. Their lives are a menagerie of conflicting personality traits, an opaque-looking glass that only reflects on itself. They understand the world and themselves only through the deep memories and forgotten truths they cannot accept. So, they create a reality in which they alone can face. For some, the past can be so horrific, so disturbing, that they cannot look at it nakedly and honestly. To do so would shatter their delicate grip on today's world. So, they walk through life in a dream of sorts, a fantasy, in which the world in their heads is the only real world, and the place outside is something to fit into that solitary make-believe place.

Karakras felt this universal truth applied here. But he was unsure how, nor did he know how to communicate with his daughter about what direction they should go. Karakras knew he needed to meditate on this more. He saw the path ahead but wasn't sure exactly where that path lay in the physical world.

Chapter 37

It was decided during the meeting that the Cereal Club did not have enough evidence to expose the tattoo owner or report him to the police yet. Yes, they uncovered evidence of a fake ID operation, but would anyone care that much? Certainly not for simple state-issued driver's licenses. But, if they could make a connection between the tattoo shop and someone inside the hospital giving them body parts and deets on dead or missing children to be used to create high-end forgeries, then they had something. Frankly, this was the whole point of Operation: Middle Finger — to find out where that poor child's finger came from and who it belonged to.

Cai was elected to do a few tasks, given her familiarity with the hospital and morgue, and because she moved like a cat when someone needed to be less-than-seen. Hudson had bought a GPS car tracker online for about ten bucks. He instructed Cai to plant it on the tattoo shop's car, under a bumper, or somewhere similar. They needed evidence that the tattoo shop was working with someone at the hospital, and this would give them tracking information on the car's whereabouts. The kids knew none of this would be admissible in court, but that didn't matter. They just wanted to get enough information to force the cops to investigate these criminals. This seemed a reasonable trade-off to them: invading someone's privacy to encourage the selective wheels of justice to grind in the right direction.

Hudson did a few days of recon on the tattoo shop to see which car belonged to the owner. It didn't take long to realize the store vehicle was the now infamous Tesla Cybertruck, one of the biggest pieces of crap ever put on

wheels, costing well over $100,000 US dollars. The truck
was wrapped with a graphic advertising The Inner Mind
Tattoo and CBD Shop.

You could tell Nico was putting his ill-gotten gains into
fancy purchases, and you could also tell that he didn't seem
to care about showing it to the authorities. Or maybe he
knew the authorities didn't care about this behavior unless
they were forced to pay attention. That didn't matter, as
the Cereal Club was about to make them pay attention to
it.

Cai easily put a tracker on the Cybertruck; she just waited
until the street looked clear. Hudson tracked the truck's
travels for the next few days. He had a map prepared for
the next meeting and showed that the Cybertruck was, in
fact, going to the hospital at least once per week.

"Now that is very curious," Hudson said, furrowing his
brow and wiping his glasses. "Why would a tattoo and CBD
store owner visit the hospital regularly?"

"It could be a simple explanation, Hudson," Sage answered.
"Maybe he has a relative or friend he is visiting?"

"Excellent point, Sage. Cai, can you investigate this further?
You know, boots on the ground and all that?"

Cai thought about it for a second. "Sure, Hud. I mean, I still
have my nurse's outfit. My Mom never took back the
master key. I guess if this is important, I can bend the rules a
bit."

"Thanks, Cai. Maybe the next time the Cybertruck heads to
the hospital, we are waiting there and follow him in to see
where he goes and what he does."

Chapter 38

According to the Cybertruck's digital tracking, on
Thursdays, right after lunch, it would go to the Old Springs
Community Hospital and stay for about 30 minutes. So,
Hudson, Cai, and Sage were waiting outside the hospital the
following Thursday. The plan was for Hudson and Sage to
stand outside as Cai, dressed in her nurse's outfit, went in
to follow Nico. The team outside would text Cai and let
her know when the truck pulled up and where, so she could
track him.

According to plan, around one p.m., the Cybertruck, blazing
its Inner Mind advertising wrap, pulled up to the hospital
entrance and drove around to the back. Really
inconspicuous stuff, thought Hudson. Hudson and Sage
walked around the side of the building to see which
entrance he was using. As they rounded the corner, they
saw an internal door with no outside handle, opening from
the inside. Hudson took a picture of the Cybertruck in the
back and a snap of Nico being let in the back door. They
immediately texted this to Cai so she could get to the
appropriate area and intercept them.

Cai hoofed it over to the back of the hospital quickly. As
she was coming around a corner, she almost bumped into
Nico and…wait one second, Cai recognized this employee
from the last time she was here. The morgue attendant who
caught Cai down in the basement during her mom's work
shift! Neither of them even noticed her; as far as they could
tell, she was just another nurse. Besides, it was apparent
they were on some important business. They crept through
the hallway with devious intent as Cai saw them go to the
main elevator that led to the basement. She waited until

they went down, then took the next elevator to the basement, lower level two, where the morgue was.

Cai's heart raced as the elevator door opened, revealing the basement's creepy glow. She vowed never to return to this floor or the morgue again, ever in her life, and yet here she was. She took a quick look to the left and the right to make sure no one was around, and, as before, it was deserted except for the flickering, disturbing glow of ancient, yellowing fluorescent lights.

Cai knew where the morgue was, and when she came to the corner right before the admission desk, she stopped in case they were still outside the room. She peeked around the corner and saw that the desk was empty as if it had been the last time she had been there. Some attendant, she thought.

Cai crept around the corner and walked up to the morgue door, which was closed and locked. She tried leaning against it to listen, but could not hear anything inside but the dim clinking hum of an air conditioner vent above her head. Well, she had a master key; she may as well use it. Very quietly, she opened the door and inched it open just an inch or two so she could see what was happening inside.

As she inched the door open, she could hear the sound of two men talking. She listened first and had her phone set to record video and audio so she could document it. She couldn't tell exactly who was saying what.

"What else do you have?"

"Check this one out; she was three," the sound of shuffling papers followed.

"That's pretty good, at least for a birth certificate or passport."

There were more sounds: a metal clicking sound followed by a metal sliding sound.

"What about this one?"

At this point, Cai knew she needed to see what they were doing. She decided to take a risk and open the door a little more to take a video of these two. As she peeked out, she could see the morgue attendant examining the finger of a young cadaver that he had just pulled out of its storage drawer. Cai didn't flinch for some reason. She was like ice and frozen. The attendant then rubbed the finger across a fingerprint ink pad and handed the pad to Nico. All of this was caught on video by Cai, whose heart was thumping out of her chest with nervousness and excitement.

Out of nowhere, a hand came down on Cai's shoulder, and she heard a familiar voice that sent her blood even more ice-cold.

"Honey bunny! What in the name of all that is Holy are you doing here?!?!"

Cai thought she was going to have a heart attack. She closed the door quietly and turned to face her mother.

Chapter 39

As Cai walked her mom away from the door and back to the elevator, she convinced her mom that she was dressed as a nurse, looking in the morgue for a bet with some other kids. She promised she would never do anything like that again, and her mother bought it and seemed to chalk it up to kids being kids and her daughter having a grim curiosity about death. Cai was lucky that the two men in the morgue didn't hear the door being closed, and she was able to get her mom out of there and back to the elevator quickly, so no one was the wiser.

Once outside, Cai found Hudson and Sage, and they walked home as she told them about her findings. Once they were back at HQ, they reviewed all the evidence in detail and were confident they had enough to expose Nico and the morgue attendant for their fake-identity business.

"Cai, this is incredible. Thank you so much." Hudson was genuinely appreciative. "And I'm sorry your mom caught you; that must not have been fun."

Cai was shaking her head sideways. "No, please, Hud, it's fine. My goal is not to lie to my mom, but this is important, and I don't want to get her involved in this and maybe lose her job or something. There is nothing the authorities would love more than to blame a working black woman for all of this. We need to keep the target on the guilty parties, not let them shift blame or accountability."

"Good points, Cai. I would not have thought of that." Hudson wasn't just being nice; Cai could see cause and effect in a way he could not. He just didn't have the life experiences she had to thread that needle.

"Here is what I was thinking of for the next steps. We follow a similar pattern to our previous cases. We have a huge online following now, and getting this case out to the right people will be easy. There are a few different angles here that will make it appealing to a wide variety of people.

"First, as we found out in our previous case, people don't like big pharma companies at all. Well, they don't seem to like hospitals very much, either. A few years ago, hospitals nationwide became for-profit; they now charge like McDonald's for basic health services, a la carte. The difference is that while you come out of a McDonald's with a Happy Meal, you leave the hospital bankrupt. They are literally fleecing people out of their life savings and generational wealth so they can get basic medical services, which in most countries are free.

"So, the first angle here is showing how horrible this hospital is and how they are not protecting their patients from exploitation and abuse. We focus on that morgue attendant and how the hospital can hire and support criminals like this.

"Next, we go against Nico and his slimy little business. Make all the focus on the fingerprints and him getting deets from dead kids so he can make high-end forgeries. No one will care about the small-time ID business once people realize this guy is stealing their dead kids' identities. That will have the parents up in arms.

"Third, we need to find some way to tie our missing finger in with Nico's operation. If it didn't come from these guys, then where?"

"It's got to be them, Hud." Cai was sure of it. "Severed kids' fingers just don't drop out of the trees. Who else can it be?"

"Yeah, but I don't want to take it to the cops, Cai. Who knows what they will do to us?" Hudson replied.

"Me neither, Hud," Cai agreed.

"Guys, we don't need to turn the finger in." Sage had a great idea. "We just fingerprint it, and then insert that fingerprint into the case file we submit online and point the police to. This way, it was just another print we took pictures of in the tattoo shop, with everything else."

"I love it. Also, Brody and I were invited into the shop; we were there by permission. I did not see any sign that pictures were not allowed, so the fact that I took some images of this public business isn't a crime." Hudson was rather proud of his ability to rationalize pretty much anything.

"Frankly, Hudson, I'm not sure taking pictures in a private hospital is legal. But then again, I'm not sure anyone is going to care when they find out what this hospital and their employees are doing to their children."

"I love this team; we have a plan!" Hudson was about to enter his sweet spot and happy place. Putting all this information into a story and presentation to move the needle on people's behavior. "I feel like we have already perfected a delivery vehicle for this type of case, and we should just reapply those processes and lessons we have learned so far. I will put together a webpage, email, text, and supporting media like advertising tiles for social media sites. Basically, a promotional and informational package about the case."

"What about another video in front of the hospital, Hudson?" Sage knew the last one had worked so well, and putting more pressure on the hospital itself after all the negative PR they got about the previous case made sense.

"That's a great idea, Sage. Unlike a webpage, the video has the potential to move organically online, so that should be the campaign's focus. We should also put together a summary video of about 15 seconds, followed by the full 2-minute video. This way, I can advertise the short segment with a small budget. And we drive people back to the webpage, which has all the contacts for the case. Of course, it all is capped with a plea to the general public to contact the local police department and the FBI to investigate this case."

"I love it, Hud," Cai said, smiling. "This way, we are not going to the police and asking for anything. John Q. public is doing it."

"Do you think we can get in trouble with the cops?" Sage was thinking aloud. "Maybe not for taking pictures in the shop, but for the hospital. It's a private business, and Cai was in a restricted area."

"Hmm. That's a good point, Sage." Hudson was wiping his glasses with his microcloth again. "Let's hope the public outrage at the hospital overshadows any attention on us. But you are right; the police may want to make an example of us for forcing them to pay attention to things they would rather ignore. We will have to take that risk if that is ok with both of you."

Sage and Cai knew they had done too much and had come too far to give up. Yes, they broke a few rules, but stopping this dreadful operation that desecrated the bodies and identities of children in the community was worth it. And as

Hudson had constantly reminded them, if other people, namely the authorities, were doing their jobs, the Cereal Club wouldn't have to do it for them.

Chapter 40

Over the past few months, Hudson had improved at putting together videos. Using basic video editing software, he learned how to create titles, transitions, and framing, and he was now even adding music and background effects.

Hudson knew what he was creating was more about propaganda than education. Propaganda is loaded information meant to influence people, whereas news is information meant to inform and educate. He wanted to influence people to call and write to the cops to get them to investigate this case. So, the material he produced was intended to do just that: agitate people's emotions to get them to take action.

Their newest video had a similar feel to their previous ones, but it was well-produced and more professional-looking. It still felt like it was put together by kids, which gave it its charm. With the new title sequence, maudlin introductory music, and text overlays that highlight the more egregious aspects of the crime, Hudson thought this was one of their most impactful videos yet. He was also getting better at cutting and intersplicing still images, graphs, and stats to bolster the story's narrative legitimacy. Hudson was behind the camera for this one, and Sage and Cai were the on-camera talent.

A gray sky. Some sad music. A camera pans down to the entrance sign of Old Springs Community Hospital, flanked on either side by our two child rights advocates.

A tear sparkles in Sage's eye as she begins, "You bring your children to The Old Spring Community Hospital to heal them. To protect them."

Then, a pan to Cai: "Sometimes, despite their best efforts, our loved ones don't always make it through life-threatening situations."

Back to Sage, "But in those challenging times, nothing is more important than to show respect to the newly deceased and their grieving families. We expect this hospital to show that respect.

"Well, our investigation found that not only are hospital employees using information from deceased children in the hospital morgue to collude with the owner of The Inner Mind Tattoo and CBD to create false IDs, they are desecrating corpses in the morgue to steal deceased children's identities."

A quick cut of the video shows the morgue attendant grabbing the cadaver's finger, with Nico clearly visible, and making a print from it.

The camera pans to Cai, with more anger now in her eyes and face than sadness, "Are your children's bodies nothing more than commodities to be used by criminal for-profit healthcare organizations?

"Are the parents of Old Springs, or the parents of America, OK with your loved ones being treated like this? Does anyone care? Will anyone do anything?"

Then displayed were images of missing children, including cases the Cereal Club had worked to solve, as well as children's fingerprints.

"Surely we can't allow this to continue?" Sage was in tears. "As children ourselves, we have done all we can to shine a light on this terrible crime. However, we need the parents and the police to help address this issue. We cannot do it alone."

Cai looked at the camera sternly. "Will you help us? Will you help these children? All it takes is a text, an email, or a phone call to the appropriate authorities. Will you fight for justice?"

The camera panned slowly, focusing on the hospital sign as text overlays appeared on the screen, including the phone number, email, and address of the Old Springs Community Police Department and the Old Springs Community Hospital. There was also contact info for the state police and the FBI, just in case the local police and hospital ignored the public outcry.

With this video in the can, Hudson felt they had the centerpiece of their marketing campaign and were about to end Nico and the hospital employees' sick business.

Chapter 41

The club was eating their daily cereal allotment when their latest video began to go viral. This was after much pushing and cajoling from Hudson and the team. They had a process and an audience now, and getting videos of child neglect to move across the global internet was a matter of course. It was all a game of how big it would get and whether the authorities would investigate and prosecute based on the evidence and the public uproar. The Cereal Club was watching the stats, shares, and likes when a familiar but unsettling bellow came up from below.

"HUDSON!"

It was not Hudson's father this time, but his big brother, Brody, who was yelling. But the tone was different, less annoyed and angrier. Shit, Hudson thought, what did I do now? He thought Brody and he had a better relationship since he helped him get his tattoo, but apparently, something had made Brody really pissed off. Before Hudson could respond, Brody bounded up the stairs and threw open the door to Hudson's bedroom.

"WHERE IS MY DRONE HUDSON?!?!" Brody was almost frothing at the mouth. No wonder, Hudson thought. Brody loved that drone; it was probably the nicest thing he had. He couldn't believe they had forgotten about it; they had been so wrapped up in Operation: Middle Finger that he had completely forgotten it was still stuck on the roof of the doctor they had briefly investigated. It took a second for Hudson to get his composure and respond to Brody, who was frankly scaring the crap out of him right now.

"Um, sorry, man, I borrowed it to record a few things and left it at my friend's house." Hudson was lying as well as he could; he wasn't a good liar.

Brody could tell he wasn't being sincere, but he didn't really care. He was so angry right now; he only wanted his drone back.

"Go and get it…NOW!" Brody yelled, walked out of the room, and slammed the door behind him. All three people in the room were dumbfounded and speechless. They had never seen such aggression towards them from such a large person, which left them unsettled.

It took a moment before Hudson could gather himself. "Well, team, it looks like we have a new sub-mission: to retrieve Brody's drone ASAP. Look, I take responsibility for this. I forgot all about it, and I am sorry you had to witness that. You did not deserve that, period."

Sage and Cai appreciated Hudson's acknowledgment, and neither blamed him. They forgot all about the drone, too.

"What's the plan, Hud?" Cai was always ready for another adventure. Besides, it would take a while to wait for the results of the fake ID investigation, so they might as well spend their time doing something productive to keep their minds busy. This may be a fun little diversion while they wait for the results of the larger case.

"Hmm, Sage, you have a good relationship with him. What do you think?"

"Well," Sage was thinking. "It's getting close to Christmas; why don't I go over and give him a present? He would love it!"

"Interesting idea," Hudson was thinking too, "and he will probably invite you in for a snack or something. What if you bring him a present, and when he invites you in, you open the back door for Cai or me so we can climb up to the roof and get Brody's drone?"

"Hud." Cai was looking at him with concern. "Why don't you let me do that? I mean, it's more up my alley." She knew Hudson was not built for that kind of work; he was more of a backroom kind of guy.

Hudson felt a little emasculated, but he had to be honest about who he was and his limitations. Cai was just more adept at this kind of action than he was.

"That makes sense, Cai, but this is no joke. I mean, we are talking about breaking and entering. I know we are just trying to get our drone back from his roof, but what we are discussing feels like a real crime."

"Look, Hud, if we don't take anything or do anything bad but retrieve our property, then it can't be that wrong. We are just going to climb up the stairs to the attic, go on the roof, get the drone, then get out of there."

Sage wasn't crazy about this plan. She liked the doctor and did not want to deceive him. "Why can't we just go to him and ask him to let us get our drone? Just tell him we were flying it, and it got stuck, and we need to get it?"

Hudson was considering, "Well, that is a good point. What worries me is that I don't trust that this doctor won't turn us in to the cops. I mean, let's say he's a good guy, and he won't, well, that's great. But I don't want to take that risk."

Cai said, "Why don't we try Hudson's plan first, and if it doesn't go as planned, then we ask him to let us retrieve it.

If we tell him about it first and he says no or turns us in, we can't get it then. Game over."

Sage and Hudson saw the logic in that.

"Ok, team, let's get this plan down to the finest detail. We need to ensure this goes smoothly so it doesn't become a bigger issue than it needs to be. We need to retrieve this property to move forward with the conclusion of Operation: Middle Finger, which is looking very good so far."

Chapter 42

After a few hours of planning, the team was ready for
Operation: Drone Retrieval. It was agreed that Hudson
would survey the house and wait for the doctor to come
home. He would then text Sage, who would walk down the
street with a Christmas present for the doctor and his
family. Sage would then try to get invited into the house
and, once in, would attempt to open a back door for Cai so
she could sneak up to the roof and retrieve the drone.
Hudson would keep an eye on everything from the tree he
had used previously and could communicate with both Sage
and Cai via text if needed.

They couldn't wait until tomorrow, as Brody was fuming.
Hudson wanted this dealt with before his father came
home, and he got in some real trouble. So, they found an
unopened bath soap set lying around Hudson's house and
wrapped it up with some leftover wrapping paper. Hudson
told Brody they were going to pick up the drone at his
friend's house and gave him the doctor's address, just so an
adult knew where they were.

Once they were close to the doctor's house, Sage waited
around the corner while Hudson climbed up the
observation tree, and Cai went around the back of the
home near the hedges. From that vantage point, she could
see if and when Sage would open the back door so she
could sprint across the yard and slip in.

Finally, they were all in position, and they waited for the
doctor to come home from work, as they had seen him do
once before. At around six p.m., the doctor's late-model
Mercedes pulled up to the large colonial house, now

decorated for Christmas with pretty white candlelight in the windows. Hudson texted Cai and Sage, letting them know the 'eagle has landed.' The doctor opened the garage and drove his car in, just as before. Hudson texted the team, "The pig is in the poke." Neither Cai nor Sage knew precisely what he meant, but they got the gist. Sage waited a minute or two for the doctor to put his bags down and say hi to his family. She then walked down the street and, after taking a big breath and calming herself, walked down the driveway to the front door. She could do this, she told herself. The front door had a large wreath, and Sage rang the bell.

Ding-dong…

A few moments later, a click is heard at the door. The door opens to a kind face, and he quickly recognizes the young girl on his doorstep.

"Why, it's Sage. Hello, young lady! What can I do for you today?" The doctor seemed really pleased to see her.

Sage put on her most adorable face, which was pretty easy as she was about as cute as possible. "Happy Holidays, doctor! I wanted to wish you a Merry Christmas and bring you this present." Sage extended the wrapped bath soap gift set.

The doctor's eyes widened, and he had a big smile. He was so pleased that this small child had remembered him and considered his feelings. "Why, that is so considerate of you, Sage. Would you come in for a cup of cocoa and meet my family?"

Sage's heart was beating hard. She smiled and nodded her head. The first step was to get in the door, and she was there. She stepped into a beautiful, higher-end home. It looked immaculate, as if it had been cleaned about three times per day. Sage wondered if the family, whom she knew was disabled and homebound, had help keeping it so clean and orderly.

There was a large wooden staircase going up to the second floor from the foyer, and down the hallway, she could see lights and hear a television from another room. Several children were talking and laughing, their voices mixed with the television. Sage calmed down a bit, being greeted by a warm home during the holidays. She could smell dinner being prepared, and was that the smell of cookies?

"Why don't you come sit down in the living room, and I'll see how my wife is doing with dinner. I'm sure she will want to meet you."

The doctor turned and started down the hall, and Sage followed him closely. As they walked the considerable distance, there were rooms to the left and right that Sage would quickly peek into as they passed. As they walked by the second room on the right, Sage could see the back of a gray-haired woman at the stove. She heard her humming a nice, quiet song to herself, apparently unaware that her husband had let someone in the house. Sage wondered if the doctor's wife was as lovely as the doctor and figured she must be.

Almost like he could read her mind, he said, "My wife is almost done with some fresh hot chocolate chip cookies. Does that sound like something you may like?"

Homemade baked cookies from a sweet old lady? Yeah, that sounded all right, thought Sage. She nodded in the affirmative with a big smile to the old doctor, who right now reminded Sage of a thinner Santa Claus. Well, maybe a little bit. She smiled again, but this time just for herself.

They continued down the hall, and Sage could now see into a room on the left where the TV was coming from. In it, she saw the back of two smaller heads sitting on a couch and watching TV, chatting and laughing over the show they were barely watching.

As if he could read Sage's mind again, Doctor Dedorius said, "Those are our two children, Macy and Lucas. Why, they must be around your age. I'll introduce you to them soon as well."

Sage thought for a moment and couldn't remember anyone with those names from school, but then she remembered their mother must have homeschooled them.

Finally, they got to the living room. The doctor motioned to Sage to the expensive-looking couch, "Please sit down for a moment and hold onto your present so you can give it to my wife. Let me go get you something to drink and check with her. What would you like?"

Sage knew the longer she could stay here, the better, as it would give Cai more time to slip in and out. "Sure, Doctor, can I have some cocoa? No sugar, please."

Doctor Dedorius smiled, "Of course, angel." Then, he wagged his finger jokingly, "You stay away from those terrible addictive substances."

Sage smiled back and waited for him to leave the room and enter the kitchen. Immediately, she jumped up and opened the latch to the back sliding door, which was only a few feet away. She returned to her seat, took out her phone, and texted Cai and Hudson, "The doors of perception are open," which was the code Hudson insisted on for when the back door was unlocked. She also texted, "All are downstairs, upstairs is empty." She wanted to let Cai know she had free rein up there for now.

Immediately, Cai sprang into action, darted across the backyard, and was at the door within a few seconds. She looked in, saw Sage on the couch, and opened the door as silently as possible. When Sage saw and heard the movement, she coughed for cover. But Sage was sure that, with the TV, the kids, the kitchen fans, and the cooking, no one would hear anything. Once inside, Cai looked to the right, saw a circular staircase heading up, and darted up without interacting with Sage. Sage just sat there, not really believing she was assisting in such an invasive act. To break into this sweet older man's house to get their drone back. Oh well, it was too late to back out now.

Chapter 43

Cai went up the stairs quickly and quietly. She had never broken into anyone's house before. Her heart was racing, and every step she made sounded so loud she thought she would be caught immediately. And the squeaks in the steps! She tried to stay at the front edge of the steps so they didn't make as much noise. It worked some. Up she went. One flight of stairs, and then there was a hallway to what looked like the main bedroom level. There was nothing of interest here for Cai. She needed to get up on the roof, whatever that meant. So up she went, continuing up the back staircase to the third floor.

This floor seemed a lot different from the last one. The first two floors were immaculate, a picture-perfect home. But this one was more cluttered. I guess that made sense, Cai thought; this was more for storage, like the basement was for poorer people's houses. Well, they probably had a basement here, too. And maybe a bowling alley, she thought, trying to calm herself with some gentle humor.

Cai walked down the third-floor hallway, and there were storage rooms to the left and right. She tried to remember where the drone was on the roof, but she didn't know exactly, so she walked into each room to look out the window to see if she could spot it. She saw nothing in the first two rooms but boxes, photo albums, dust, and other old stuff. But when she got to the third room on the street side, she saw something through the frosted window panes. Was that a metallic or plastic glimmer? Cai crept into the room, peeked through the window, and saw Brody's drone on the roof, nestled between the eave and the window. Cai looked at the window, and it seemed it hadn't been opened in about thirty years. It may have even been painted shut. But how else was she going to get out there? It made sense to try to open this window.

She knew she had to do this quietly but also quickly. Cai had no idea how long Sage could keep the family busy downstairs, and getting arrested for B&E was not on her Christmas schedule. She saw a small step ladder in the corner of the room and put it next to the window so she could stand on it and get better leverage. First, she flipped the latch on the window and tried to lift it. It would not budge. So, she stopped, got a better grip, and then pushed even harder. Still, no luck. Not even a little movement. Shit, thought Cai. Was she going to need a tool here? She decided to try it once more and then devise a new plan. She put all her weight and strength behind it and pushed up with all her might. Her hand slipped off the window frame; she lost her balance, fell off the ladder, and came crashing to the ground. Knocking paint cans and skis over in the process caused an enormous racket. One that Cai was sure would bring the homeowner to investigate.

Chapter 44

Sage didn't hear Cai's ruckus upstairs. The sounds of a happy family at Christmas time were enough to drown out any noise from two flights up. Sage was so nervous she worried the doctor would notice when he returned. She tried to calm and steady herself with a breathing exercise she had learned. It worked a little bit. Just then, the doctor returned from the kitchen.

"Sage, thank you so much for waiting. I was talking to my wife. Would you like to have dinner with us? You can call your parents to let them know you are staying a little while."

Sage was a little shocked; she didn't expect this. But why didn't she? They were friendly people, and inviting her to dinner was the decent thing to do. From an operational point of view, this was a good thing since it would give Cai more time to retrieve the drone and get out. But what would Sage's parents say? She never told her mom or dad that she was coming here. She wondered if telling them would compromise the operation and get Hudson or Cai in trouble. She wasn't sure what to do. She was going to have to think on her feet.

"That is so nice of you and your wife, doctor. Sure, that would be great. Let me text my mom and tell her I'll stay for dinner."

The doctor was visibly pleased, "Oh, that is wonderful, sweetheart. Let me tell my wife to set another place at the dining room table, and we will be ready to eat in about 15 minutes. Do you need anything else while you are waiting? How about some cookies?"

"That would be amazing. Thank you, doctor."

The doctor returned to the kitchen to assist his wife, and Sage texted her mom, Alona. She mostly told the truth: that she dropped off a Christmas present at their doctor's, and they invited her to stay for dinner. Her mom texted back that it was fine, but to please let her know earlier next time, as it would be more considerate. Phew, Sage thought, that was a close one. She then texted both Hudson and Cai to let them know she was going to have dinner with the family and not to worry about how long she would be in there. Hudson replied quickly, thanking her for the update, but Sage never got a reply from Cai. She wondered if everything was OK with her.

Chapter 45

Cai was lying in a pile of clothes, boxes, and rags after falling off the step ladder while trying to open the window. She was so jacked up from anxiety and nervousness that she tried to push too hard and made a much bigger racket than she expected. Cai was sitting in the pile, waiting for some adult to come in and all hell to break loose. But after a minute or two, no one came. She wondered if they even heard it. Cai knew she couldn't wait around forever to find out. She needed to get that drone and get the hell out of there.

First things first. She had to open that window or find another way to get out on the roof. She looked closer at the window to see if she could pry it open with a screwdriver or something. Using her cell phone light, she could see now that the window was indeed painted shut, and there was no way she was getting it open. She could have avoided the fall if she had only moved more deliberately and looked more closely before acting. Cai needed to remember to look before jumping in too fast in the future.

She was going to have to find a different way onto the roof. Looking for another window made the most sense, so she backtracked one room toward the stairs she had come up initially. It was another messy storage-type room, with paint cans and wood and other things kids really couldn't care less about. She carefully stepped over them to ensure she did not make a racket again and scrutinized the window closely this time. She was lucky it was not painted shut.

Cai returned to the other room, got the step ladder, and positioned it near the new window. She got a good grip and tried to move the window. It did not budge. For the first time, Cai got scared that she might be unable to complete her mission. She needed to try again and put some weight into it. She feared falling again, but Cai had come too far now. She pushed, and there was finally some movement, just a little bit. It was enough to loosen it up. She stopped for a moment, caught her breath, and then gave it one good last push, and the window finally came up, with a blast of cold air hitting her in the face.

Cai looked outside to see what she was up against. First, she could see the tree Hudson was in across the street, but she couldn't see Hudson. Just as she had that thought, she saw a light flash from the tree and figured Hudson was flashing his phone light. Well, that's good, Cai thought. If I fall, at least someone will call an ambulance.

She looked down and got a little frightened. This was pretty high up. The roof was slanted, but not too much at this point, and she could see the drone several steps away to the right. She could imagine herself getting there if she leaned on the house to steady herself, but getting back with the drone was going to be an issue. If she carried it, she could not lean or balance properly and could fall. What was Cai going to do? She stopped to think for a second. Jeez, this was getting more stressful and difficult by the second. She wanted to help Hudson, but she did not want to hurt herself. She was going to have to balance the two. She texted Hudson,

"Hud, on my right, about 10 ft. Have to go across a slanted roof. Don't think I can get back with a drone. Maybe have to toss it down into the bushes. That OK with U?" Cai then waited, not knowing how much Hudson was freaking out right now.

The thought of potentially breaking his brother's expensive gadget was freaking Hudson out. He thought it through. If she tried to bring it back, she and the drone could fall, which would be very bad. If she threw it down to him, he probably couldn't just catch it, which could break his finger or arm. If she threw it down into that nice flat bush there, it might be OK. So, on further reflection, her suggestion made a lot of sense.

Hudson texted back, "Np Cai, that is a good plan. Just try to hold it flat and drop it so it lands even on the bush below U."

Cai got ready to go out the window. She looked at the ledge she would step on and saw it was slanted. So, she put her first leg over the windowsill, then the other, keeping her arm on the sill. As she put pressure on the first leg on the roof, she could feel that it was rough, and her foot had a good grip. Cai then put her other foot down on the roof, which she had overlooked had black ice on it, and her foot slipped, then her other foot slipped, and then Cai screamed.

Chapter 46

For the first time, Sage noticed that it was taking Cai a long time, or at least it seemed that way, and she started to get a little concerned. It was possible Cai had found another way out, but doubtfully. She would need to return through this back staircase, and Sage was sitting a few feet from it. Maybe it was just taking longer than expected. If another person had gone upstairs, they would have sounded the alarm, and so far, Sage had heard and seen nothing unusual. Everyone was having a nice night. Almost on her thought, the doctor returned to the room with a plateful of homemade chocolate chip cookies, and Sage forgot all about Cai for a moment.

"Doctor, thank you so much. They look AMAZING!" Sage meant it; they looked almost like they were out of a picture or advertisement. They smelled incredible, too.

The doctor smiled, proud of his wife's culinary creation, "Of course, Sage! She has entered them in several local, state, and even national competitions, so she is very proud of them. Please take as many as you want."

Sage wanted more, but she didn't want to be rude. They were going to have dinner, so she only took one. Then, she looked to the doctor to see if he was disapproving, and he wasn't, so she took another. The doctor didn't make a snide comment like other adults would about taking too many. Sage liked that about him. She was respectful and not piggish, and he was kind and respectful in return.

"I hope you enjoy them, Sage." The doctor now had an apron on. "We should have dinner ready in about fifteen minutes. Feel free to watch TV or do whatever while you wait."

"I have my phone, doctor, not a problem. I'm playing a few games and chatting with some friends," which was all true, obviously omitting the part about her being a distraction to keep the Dedorius family busy. In contrast, her friends got their expensive property back. The doctor quickly left the room to help his wife prepare the rest of the meal.

Chapter 47

Hudson almost fell out of the tree when he saw Cai slip. He felt totally responsible for her being up there, and, frankly, he should have gone himself instead of putting her in danger. Here he was, sitting up in a tree doing nothing while his two female friends took all the risks. He felt helpless. Hudson was about to jump down and try to catch Cai from her fall when she got her grip and steadied herself.

Hudson wanted to text or call Cai, but knew he couldn't. Just let her do her job; that is what he told himself to stay in his place. He could see she had regained her footing and was starting to edge across the slanted roof while leaning on the side of the house for balance. Hudson decided it would be best to get down under where she was, so when she threw the drone down, he was there to retrieve it. So, he climbed down the tree, made sure no one was around, and made his way across the lawn to the bushes near the house under Cai and the drone.

Hudson whispered up to Cai, "Hey, it's me. Don't worry. I am down here if you need anything. Just hang tight and drop it right down when you're ready."

Cai felt much better knowing there was a friend and some support close. Even if Hudson couldn't do anything beyond calling for help, at least someone who cared was nearby.

"Thanks, Hud, I got this." She could do this.

Cai inched further to the right. After her foot slipped on the black ice, she checked each step to ensure she wouldn't slip again. She grabbed onto gutters or anything else she could so she wouldn't fall off the roof if she slipped again. Step by step, she went on, with Hudson staying right under her for support, trying to keep his mouth shut.

Finally, after what seemed like hours but was only a few minutes, Cai reached the area where the drone was, nestled between the eave of the house and an arch. It wasn't something you could see from the street, which is why no one ever noticed it, but once at the right vantage point, it was easy to see and access.

Cai secured both her feet—one on the roof and another on the arch above the second-floor window. She looked down first to reconnect with Hudson visually and see where to drop the drone. Hudson was right below her and, as if reading her mind, pointed to a flat hedge bush that looked like it would provide a soft landing for the sensitive drone.

As Cai reached for the drone, a set of car LED high beams hit them as they came around a corner. Hudson was so freaked out that he dove into the bushes while Cai crouched behind the window. Soon, the car passed by without slowing, and Hudson popped up from the bush. And Cai couldn't help but suppress a laugh, seeing Hudson all messed up. It helped to lighten the mood a bit, which was way too tense.

Cai relaxed her body, grabbed the drone, and softly dropped it onto the flat bush top, where Hudson was waiting to grab it.

Chapter 48

"The eagle has landed on the moon! The eagle has landed!" Hudson was texting Sage excitedly, letting her know they had the drone. Sage couldn't be happier, but now that she had agreed to stay for dinner, she was not in a hurry anymore. At least that was done, and she no longer worried about it. But she had not seen Cai come down the stairs yet, so either she found another way out or dropped the drone so she didn't have to lug it through the house.

She texted both of them to make sure, "Is the eagle leaving the nest soon?" Sage didn't have Hudson's flair for codenames, but she was doing her best.

Hudson was the first to reply, "Yes, we had to improvise. The eagle is on its way."

Sage was happy about that, too. Once Cai was out of there, she didn't have much to worry about. Mission accomplished! And even better, they were in the final stages of Operation: Middle Finger and should soon see police action against the hospital and tattoo shop. She just needed to wait here until Cai came down, then eat a few bites, and she was out of there. Just then, the doctor came back into the room.

"Sage, are you ready for dinner? My wife has been preparing all day, and I can't wait for you to meet my family."

Damn, Sage thought. She wanted to wait until Cai came down and saw her out, but didn't see any way to delay dinner. She had been here for about twenty minutes already. Sage had already finished the cookies and was pretty psyched for a good home-cooked meal. She loved her mom's cooking, but she made more traditional vegetarian indigenous foods, while here, there was a real US Thanksgiving dinner, hopefully with turkey and everything. Sage didn't usually eat meat, but maybe she could make an exception tonight.

Sage got up to follow the doctor to the dining room. They went back down the main hallway they had initially come through, passing the kitchen on the left and the TV room on the right, which were both empty and quiet. As they approached the dining room, Sage could see that all the lights were turned down, and there were candles lit. Cool, thought Sage; she loved candles. She could tell some were scented candles, giving off a strong Christmas pine vibe. She could also hear the two children chattering back and forth, and the mother quietly chided them to keep their manners in mind during dinner.

As they walked into the dining room, Sage saw the doctor's wife at one end of the table and their two children at the other. There was a placemat for Sage on the other side of the table, and the doctors were set opposite his wife. Sage took her place.

After she sat down, it was the first time Sage noticed it was really dark in the dining room. The candlelight created a good atmosphere, but didn't give quite enough light to eat and converse. It was so dark that she had trouble making out the kids' and the doctor's wife's faces. She could see faint outlines, but nothing was defined. Their conversation continued like she wasn't even there.

The doctor began, "Family, we are so lucky to have a guest here for our holiday celebration. So please take a moment to say hello to Sage!"

Just then, there was a click, and the mother and children immediately stopped their conversations. At this moment, Sage realized she felt a little sleepy for the first time in the evening.

Chapter 49

Cai saw Hudson pick up the drone, give it a quick once-over, and then signal to her that all was well with a thumbs-up sign. Cai saw Hudson run across the street, stash the drone in a different bush, and climb back up the tree to his original position.

Cai slowly etched her way back to the window and climbed in without much trouble. Once inside, she spent a few minutes putting everything back where it was so it wouldn't be obvious to anyone in the house that anything was amiss.

As she was straightening up, Cai found a bound book of family photos lying on the ground. This was strange, she thought; few moms would let something like this lie around on the ground in a storage area like this. Cai knew she had to get out of there quickly, but her curiosity got the best of her, and she opened the photo album.

At first look, it seemed like a regular photo album, with everything from baby pictures to family photos on holidays and other significant events, like opening Christmas presents. Then, of course, there were all those day-to-day pictures, quick snaps from daily events like playing in the yard and bar-b-qing in the backyard. All the family was there: the doctor, his beautiful wife, and their two cute kids, all blond and Aryan-looking.

After Cai flipped through the picture album, something struck her as a little weird. The album hadn't been filled out yet, as people usually fill them out thoroughly and then go on to the next one. All the pictures, which could be dated from date stamps on some of the images, were from about ten or fifteen years ago. And the album was only about half full. It was like a family frozen in time, a snapshot of happiness. Then she remembered when they first looked into the doctor as a person of interest; he and his whole family had been involved in a catastrophic car collision about ten years ago.

 Ah, there were no pictures of him or his family after the accident. Maybe the reality is too painful for him and his wife. To take photos of a family that is now homebound and disabled. Just remember the way things used to be before everything went sideways. Cai understood that. There are some things in the world you want to forget and avoid. A horrific accident that took away this beautiful family and turned them into something different is just what a man and woman may want to not record in pictures.

Cai felt sympathy and compassion for the doctor and his family. What must they have gone through? What are they still going through? She then realized she had been in there too long and began descending the back stairs to reconnect with Hudson.

Chapter 50

Sage was waiting for the family to respond to the doctor's invitation to welcome her, but she didn't hear anything. Each family member was completely still and silent.

She wondered why they weren't answering him when the doctor spoke again. "Now, now, don't be shy, everyone. Macy and Lucas, why don't you tell Cai all about your school day?"

Sage patiently waited for the kids to talk. Nothing happened. They didn't fidget, move around, or say a word.

She was about to ask them a further question to see if she could get them to talk when the doctor started again. "That's wonderful, Macy! I know how much you love your science teacher. It's so different for a young girl to enjoy science, isn't it, Sage?"

Sage didn't understand what the doctor was talking about. Did he hear something she couldn't hear? She just nodded, not sure what to say exactly.

"What about you, Lucas?" The doctor continued. "How was soccer practice today?" Then, over to Sage. "Sage, Lucas was the top scorer on his team this year. They may be giving him an award at the annual convention."

Even though it was dark in the dining room, Sage could tell the doctor was beaming with pride. She still didn't get what was happening, seeing as the kids weren't saying anything as far as she could tell. So, she decided to play along; maybe she wasn't getting something here.

"Um, that's amazing, doctor," Sage kept her head down. She was definitely feeling tired. Maybe she should go home a little earlier than expected. "Good for you, Lucas," she said a bit weakly.

"Honey," the doctor was now verbally projecting more, apparently talking to his wife at the end of the table. "What is this wonderful meal we are about to eat?"

Sage looked over at the mother, who was as still and motionless as the kids. She strained to listen, as maybe they whispered something only the doctor could hear. She heard nothing.

After a short delay, the doctor continued, "Oh, that is wonderful! There is nothing like Christmas ham, huh, Sage? I hope you are not a vegetarian. Are you sweetie?"

Sage was most definitely a vegetarian, but she wanted to be polite, "Why yes, doctor, I am a vegetarian. I'm sure some salad and sides will be fine for me. I'm so sorry, Mrs. Dedorius. I'm sure the ham is delicious." The doctor's wife remained still and did not react.

Sage's head felt really…heavy. Like she had been up late watching a movie. She thought it sure was dark here, which must be making her sleepy.

"Do you think we will be eating soon, doctor?" Sage struggled to keep her eyes open, hoping food would pep her up. But frankly, this was way too weird; maybe she should be going now. But getting up seemed almost impossible with how tired she was.

"Oh, Sage, we have so much to discuss first. This is more than just a dinner. This is an invitation!' The doctor sounded brimming with excitement. "We want you to join our family and be one of us! Would you like that, Sage?"

Before Sage could answer or even really comprehend what he just said, her head became so heavy that she could no longer keep it up, and it dipped down softly till it hit the table. The doctor smiled, pleased that the evening was going so well. His wife and family must be so proud of him, he imagined.

Chapter 51

Karakras, the Shuar uwishin, and Sage's father came out of his meditation in a sweat. He was violently shaking and in complete horror. How could he have been so blind? How did he not see what was being presented to him by the Sentinel right in front of his eyes? He, like many travelers into the fabric of the broader universe, overanalyzed and overthought the visions he had. He dove too deep into the mystique and aura of the infinitely complex and unknowable. He sought paths in too many directions and looked for far-flung subtlety when he needed to look closer to home.

Karakras jumped to his feet. He didn't know how much time he had, just that he had made possibly the biggest mistake of his life. He ran around the house screaming for his wife, Alona. He found her outside in the vegetable garden.

"Alona, please forgive me. But I have made a terrible mistake." Karakras was so upset that he was still shaking. He was almost in shock. Alona had never seen her husband like this. He was always so strong and steady. Something was really wrong.

"My love!" Alona tried to comfort her shaken husband. "What mistake could you have made that could be so terrible?" She truly did not understand his consternation.

Karakras looked deeply into his wife's eyes. In a near trance, he spoke slowly, "The nature of the beast I could not see because he hides so clearly on a plain day. He walks and talks with impunity, even in his own mind. That is what I could not grasp. I was looking for the mind of a monster;

instead, I needed to be looking for the mind inside the monster."

Alona had no idea what he was talking about. She knew it was about a vision, but she was not sure which one. She decided to let him continue, hoping it would make sense soon.

"He is so close; he always was so close. A sinister presence. Now that I see under the mask, I can feel him permeating the neighborhood. I feel it as his deranged sickness pervades this town."

Alona was getting scared. Who was he talking about? She finally had to say something,

"Who, Karakras? Who is this beast you speak of? Was this a vision you had?"

Her voice helped to jog Karakras back into semi-reality, out of his trance. "Yes! A vision. I had brought a finger with me. I tried to perform the penke karamprar ritual to commune with the spirit of the finger." Karakras was talking more excitedly; he was visibly sweating. "I was confused because the finger spirit thought it was still alive. That it was living a normal life and had not lost its finger. This confused me, so I thought the spirit was playing psychological games with me. But I didn't conceptualize that the spirit itself could be delusional. That it thought it was still alive when it was not."

It was starting to make sense to Alona. This was the finger that Sage and her friends had given Karakras. She had thought little of it before. Now, alarm bells were going off in her head. How was this connected to her daughter?

"Karakras, you need to tell me right now. Does this have anything to do with our daughter, Sage?" Alona was shaking her husband, trying to jolt him into coherence.

His eyes widened. "Yes, my love, I am afraid it does." Karakras had his head down; he was deeply ashamed. He had failed his family.

Just then, a light went off in Alona's head. The call from Sage. She was having dinner with someone, a person they trusted implicitly. But surely that didn't have anything to do with this horrific vision the uwishin had? With that finger, he tried to commune with?

"We must get our daughter Karakras! RIGHT NOW!"

"Alona, we need assistance." Karakras was regaining his composure and was acting like the father and protector he had always been. "This may be beyond something just you and I can handle. We need support, and I do not trust the police or the authorities."

Alona nodded her head in agreement. "Our overlords do not want justice or equality for us, only subservience and silence. They are just as likely to attack our daughter and us as protect her from one of their own."

"You speak the truth, my love. We must ensure the safety of our daughter before alerting the authorities to the crimes of this man. We don't want her caught in their crossfire." Karakras' mind was working more clearly now. "I will call on my closest spirit travelers to assist us. We must move quickly."

Chapter 52

Cai descended the back stairs easily enough. Luckily for her, no one had come upstairs in the half hour she was trying to get the drone. She felt like their operation was almost over and a complete success if she did say so herself. The fact that Cai went out on that roof, kept her shit together, and retrieved the drone successfully and without damage made her quite proud. The fact that she could help Hudson, who was quickly becoming one of her favorite people, made her even happier.

As Cai approached the main level, she peeked around the corner of the stairs to see if Sage was still sitting on the couch. She noticed she was no longer there and figured that made sense since Sage had told them she would be having dinner with the family. On the way to the sliding door, Cai heard some conversation coming down the hallway. Hmm, she thought, maybe she should check on Sage quickly to make sure she is OK. So, she inched her way down the hallway a few steps, just enough to be able to hear and peek into the candle-lit dining room. Cai could see that Sage was having a nice dinner with the doctor and his family. People were chatting, and all seemed well.

Convinced that Sage was safe and having fun, Cai backed down the hallway and into the living room. She slid out the sliding door and closed it, leaving it unlocked behind her. She didn't think you could lock a sliding door from the outside anyway, so she left it open. Hopefully, the family wouldn't notice, or Sage could lock it again on her way out. Cai reminded herself to text Sage to do that when she was back with Hudson.

Within thirty seconds, Cai was across the backyard, through the shrubs, and at the bottom of the tree Hudson was keeping watch in. She shimmied up much quicker than Hudson did and patted him on the back.

"Is the drone OK?" Cai asked right away.

"It's fine," Hudson confirmed. "Thanks so much for doing that, Cai. I couldn't have done it without you." Hudson meant it, too. He knew he was limited in his ability to accomplish specific tasks, and Cai was adept at filling in where he was lacking.

Cai appreciated Hudson's acknowledgment. "Thanks, Hud. It felt pretty good to go out on the edge like that and not choke."

"I think we should wait here for Sage until she is done." Hudson was trying to think about others and be empathetic, something he had learned from Sage. "Just to make sure she is safe and see her home."

"Agreed, Hud. Let's text her and tell her we will be here waiting for her."

"Done," Hudson replied.

Chapter 53

Sage never saw Hudson's text. After she had passed out, drugged from the cookies she had eaten, she slipped into a black hole of nothingness.

The doctor was exceedingly happy with how well the evening was going. He had introduced his family to Sage, and they seemed to get on well. His children and wife really took to her, and it wasn't as uncomfortable as he thought it might be. His family wasn't always so communicative, given they had been homebound for over a decade, and to see them light up when a new person came over was encouraging to him. How long had it been since he had someone new over for his family to meet? It had been some time, that was for sure.

It felt different with Sage. She was such a good person, so compassionate and empathetic for such a young girl. He thought it was rare for a child to have so much emotional intelligence. Those qualities were sorely missing in his family. They were too focused on their own needs.

After the pleasantly successful dinner, the doctor felt confident it would all work out fine. His house felt more alive and vibrant with Sage than in years. The doctor felt invigorated and was ready to take on the next phase of his life's journey. With his family by his side, he knew he had the foundation to accomplish almost anything. His calling was to serve humankind and be a guiding light for them, a sort of moral compass, he hoped. The doctor's healing hands and steady countenance were the anchors on which he based his life.

It took some time for the doctor to move everyone into the basement for the procedure. He had learned that it was a good thing when everyone was involved in the process; it made it more of a family event, giving them the time together that they needed to grow as a family unit. These were the tentpoles that a family needed, he reflected pensively.

Since the accident, he had spent years equipping his house for his home-bound family. The doctor wanted to ensure he had the necessary medical facilities and equipment so he would not have to take them to the hospital for every minor issue. He brought Sage down first and set her on the metal examination table, similar to the one Cai had seen in the morgue at the Old Springs Community Hospital. In fact, that is where the doctor got his, along with much of his equipment. Oh, all legally, of course. The doctor was no thief. He bought everything second-hand as the hospital was upgrading to other equipment.

He then set up chairs for his family around the metal table and helped them get down the stairs and into position. Whew, it was a lot of work, the doctor thought. But it was all worth it. Yes, his family had been impacted by the accident, but they were all still alive, and he cherished every minute they had together. What a blessing, he reflected.

Oops, one more thing. The doctor made sure to secure Sage's arms and legs with restraints softly. Just for safety's sake, he thought lovingly. Don't worry, Sage, he whispered to her; it will all be over soon.

Chapter 54

It took about thirty minutes for Karakras and Alona to gather their fellow Shuar tribesmen and women. In total, they had about six warriors to assist in rescuing Sage. They hoped this would be enough. They had no idea what they would find beyond what Karakras had gleaned from his vision. He knew time was short, and the danger to Sage was great, so they needed to move quickly.

The Shuar equipped themselves with their traditional weaponry, as they would have on any mission or hunting expedition. Included were several warriors with Shuar tantar shields and nanki lances. These warriors would provide support and cover from the bushes on the sides of the house. Both Karakras and Alona were armed with Shuar blowguns equipped with tunta arrows, which were themselves dipped in a poison that would paralyze a human but not kill them. A few Shuar came dressed in traditional hunting gear, while others dressed in dark outfits that would blend with the night as they provided guard.

The plan was for Karakras and Alona to try to get Sage away from the house. Peacefully, if possible, or by force, if necessary. Two warriors would wait out back for cover and support, while two would wait out front. Karakras and Alona would knock on the door and go from there. Alona had already tried texting Sage repeatedly and was not getting a response. She was getting more nervous by the minute and was pushing the rest of the response team to move as fast as possible.

Soon, they pulled up in front of the Dedorius family home in two older-model cars and parked on the street. As planned, the Shuar warriors got out of one car while two blended into the bushes in front of the home; the other two went around the house to stand guard over the backyard. They moved silently and stealthily.

Next, Karakras and Alona got out, leaving their weapons in the car for now. They planned just to knock first and ask for Sage. Why make it more complicated than that? They were here to pick up their daughter from dinner, no big deal.

They approached the door and rang the bell. No answer. They rang the bell again. Again, no answer. They waited a few moments and knocked on the door. No answer. They knocked again. Again, no answer. They were about to retreat to the car and formulate a plan when they heard a whistling from the tree. Karakras and Alona looked up to clearly see Hudson and Cai in the tree, waving their arms and trying to whistle to get their attention.

Chapter 55

Sage felt unbelievably terrible. She had never felt like this before, but she imagined getting punched in the head or having a large rock dropped on you was equivalent. She hadn't even tried to open her eyes. Sage knew that opening them meant she would have blinding light in her eyes, and this would make the dull thud in her head turn into a thunderous roar. But she didn't have much of a choice. She may as well be in a hospital, given how she felt. Perhaps it was time to check.

Slowly, she opened her eyes, and it wasn't easy. They were almost crusted shut, like she was so dehydrated her eyes were fused. Oh, that was it; she needed water! She had never been so thirsty in her life. Sage opened her eyes a little more and saw she definitely was not at home. It looked like she was in a hospital or a doctor's office. Above, Sage saw an overhead light like in a doctor's examination room. Around her were metal trays full of mysterious equipment she didn't fully understand. She was confused for sure, but she must have gotten hurt or passed out and was at a facility.

But wait one second, Sage couldn't move her legs or arms. Was the accident worse than she thought? With an extreme headache, she inched her head up to see that both her arms were strapped to the table with leather straps. She couldn't lift her head enough to see if her legs were restrained similarly, but Sage assumed they were done like her arms. She tried to look to either side, but her view was blocked by all the equipment and trays around her. Until someone came to loosen her straps, she was not moving.

Just then, she heard a familiar voice, "Ah, Sage, are you awake? Oh, good, I didn't want you to miss all of this!" The doctor seemed very happy and excited, which immediately made Sage feel better. If she were really sick, then he would sound worried or concerned.

"Oh, doctor," Sage could hear her voice slurring. " Did something happen? Where am I?"

The doctor spoke in a calming voice: "Now, Sage, you are just fine. I am so sorry for any discomfort you may be experiencing. But I don't want you to worry. I've talked to my family, and they all absolutely LOVE you and want you to join us."

What was he talking about? Sage thought, "I'm sorry, doctor, I'm a little confused. What do you mean, your family wants me to join them?"

The doctor seemed genuinely surprised, "Oh, I apologize for jumping ahead. I can see the medication may have affected your memory. During our dinner, we all had a very engaging conversation, and we all, including you, made an important decision."

Sage couldn't imagine what he was talking about; she didn't remember any conversation. She just sat down for dinner, and the next thing she knew, she woke up here.

The doctor waited for Sage to respond, and when she didn't, he continued excitedly, "You are going to be part of our family, Sage!" The doctor waited a moment for a look of joy to come over Sage's face, and when it didn't, he said, "We have been looking for a new member of our family for some time, and you are it!"

Sage didn't understand at all. She had a family. She was very happy there. Why would the doctor think that she wanted a different family?

Just then, the doctor swung the table she was strapped to around to face the opposite direction, and Sage could see three people sitting in chairs in a semicircle facing her table. She was groggy, and her head hurt, but she did her best to focus on them.

Like when they were up in the dining room, the three people were completely motionless. Sage could now see what they were wearing, and she could now make out their faces and their hands. They looked…dried out, like a raisin or a dried prune or something. Their eyes looked…weird, like glassy and still. They didn't blink or move them at all. Just then, Sage noticed the smell. She didn't know what it was, but it was old, musty, and gross.

"Sage, you remember my wife and kids from dinner!" The doctor sounded beyond excited, almost ecstatic. "Honey and kids, please welcome our newest family member!"

At that moment, Sage's brain kicked in and made connections it didn't want to make. She was looking not at three healthy and living people, but at three desiccated corpses.

Chapter 56

Hudson and Cai were shocked when they saw the two older cars pull up in front of the Dedorius house. They had no idea what was happening, so they just waited to see. First, they saw two people get out of one car and run around the side of the house. Then, they saw two more get out of the same vehicle and hide in the bushes in front. If he wasn't mistaken, it looked to Hudson like they were all armed with spears and shields. Hudson had to do a double-take. Is that really what he saw? He looked at Cai as if to silently say WTF?

After a few moments, someone stepped out of the other car, and it didn't take long for both Hudson and Cai to realize it was Sage's parents, Karakras and Alona. Holy shit, what were they doing here? As far as they knew, Sage was having dinner, had asked for permission, and all was fine. And now, here come two cars screeching up to the house, and her parents are walking up to the front door.

Hudson and Cai decided to wait to see what happened before exposing themselves.

"Cai, we should check on Sage and let her know her parents are here."

"I'm on it, Hud." Cai was already sending the text out.

Karakras and Alona went to the door and rang the bell a few times. They then knocked on the door several times, and there was no response. Not a peep or any sight of movement in the home. Wow, that was weird, thought Hudson. Why wouldn't the doctor or a member of his family answer the door? Even during dinner, they would still respond, he thought.

"Any response, Cai?"

"Nothing, Hud." Cai was getting worried, too. "Maybe we should jump down and chat with her parents? Just tell them we were waiting for her; we don't need to mention the drone mission."

Hudson nodded his head in agreement. He then tried to whistle. It wasn't easy. He thought he could whistle, but it wasn't very loud. Luckily, Cai joined in, and between their sad whistles and waving their arms, Karakras and Alona saw them and were just as shocked to see Sage's close friends hanging out in a tree.

Chapter 57

Sage felt like she should have been in shock from seeing three long-dead bodies sitting in front of her, all dressed up in their Sunday finest. She was freaked out, but no more than when they first saw the missing finger they had been investigating. Maybe it was the drugs she ingested or the fact that she was getting more desensitized to violence and bizarre events, and just didn't react as strongly anymore.

She tried to get more alert. Yup, those were dead bodies. She had seen them on TV lots of times; no mistake there. And they were all dressed up nicely, like it was a holiday dinner. That was weird, she thought. Why were they dressed up like they were still alive? Sage's question would get answered relatively quickly.

"What was that, honey?" Sage could hear no sound or question. The doctor seemed to be hearing something Sage could not. "I'm not sure. Sage, my wife, wants to know what your favorite class in school is?"

Sage looked at the doctor's face to see if he was joking or putting her on. He was not. He seemed normal and at ease, just like they were at an annual physical check-up. Sage did not know exactly what to do here. Just play along until she could get some more information, she thought.

"Um, I really like history, ma'am."

"Oh, that is amazing, Sage," the doctor said, nodding his head in excitement. "We don't have any real history buffs in the family! Right, honey?"

What was he talking about with this 'in the family' stuff? It probably made sense for Sage to suss that out first.

"Thank you so much, doctor, but I already have a family."

The doctor's mask of well-being fell away for the first time, and underneath, there was nothing more than a blank stare. When Sage looked into his eyes, they seemed so black, so empty. Infinitely deep and void of everything. This was not the nice doctor she knew and trusted. Who was this man?

It took the doctor some time to respond. It was almost like Sage had broken something in him. When he spoke again, he was more like the nice doctor she knew, but she could still see this other empty person there, which really scared her.

"No, no, Sage, you are remembering your old life. Those times are long gone now. Your family is here now. Your new mother is here, and your new siblings are here. Don't you want to make them happy and become a part of something bigger than yourself?"

Sage didn't know what to say. She was beginning to realize the doctor was more than just a little unhinged. She thought she should agree with him for now. She needed more information first.

"Sure, doctor, that sounds great." Her response had its desired effect, and the doctor perked up immediately. "Is the room we are in at your office? I don't recognize it."

The doctor looked around, pleased with his handiwork. "Oh no, Sage, this is my personal medical facility. I use this to help keep my family in tip-top shape. Could you imagine how much trouble it would be to take them all to the hospital for every little issue? When you have a home-bound family, you must improvise and innovate!"

"It must be difficult, doctor." Sage was cautious about what she said now, after seeing that horrible look on his face. "To have all that responsibility on your shoulders."

The doctor looked as if he were about to cry, but then he caught himself and regained his composure. "It is challenging, Sage, but it is so rewarding. When you spend your life as a healer for others, turning those talents towards home and supporting my family like I do is more than I could ever have asked for." He reflected momentarily, "I am so fortunate to have the resources and ability to keep my family safe and growing."

"It is quite the facility, doctor." Sage was emotionally intelligent enough to know a man like the doctor needed to be complimented. His ego demanded it. "What kind of procedures can you do here?"

The doctor's eyes lit up with Sage's inquiry, "Sage, what an insightful question! Why, I can do pretty much anything you can do in a hospital. From minor procedures to more major ones. You can see we are fully equipped here to manage a full family indefinitely!"

Sage didn't want to ask the following question, but felt she had to: "What kind of procedure are we doing today, doctor?"

The doctor smiled and patted Sage on the head, "Now, don't worry your pretty little head about that, Sage. I am a professional with years of training and experience, and you can trust me." The doctor then ensured Sage's straps were tight on her legs and arms.

Chapter 58

Hudson and Cai didn't take long to inform Sage's parents about their situation. They fibbed a bit and didn't mention that they were sneaking into these people's homes to get their drone back. They said they were waiting for Sage, who had stopped to say hello. When Sage texted her parents and them that she would stay for dinner, they decided to wait for her and walk her home. Neither Hudson nor Cai knew that Sage was in any danger.

After listening patiently, Karakras quickly updated Sage's friends about his concerns. Both of them could tell by the gravity of his voice and the seriousness of his composure that he was not overstating his worry. There was something very wrong in that house, and they had to go in immediately to ensure Sage was safe. Cai let Karakras and Alona know that the back sliding door was open and where the dining room was in the house. Karakras looked at her momentarily, wondering exactly how she would know those details, but he didn't bother saying anything. More important things were afoot; they needed to move quickly and decisively.

Karakras instructed Hudson and Cai to wait out front for them and to stay on their phones if either he or his wife needed to contact them. He and Alona equipped themselves with their blowguns and set their phones to record audio and video so they could document everything that went down. Then Hudson interjected, suggesting they livestream themselves so the rest of the team could monitor their progress. Karakras had no idea how to do that, so within a minute, Hudson had set up live streaming from his and Alona's phones. Karakras had a clip on his belt to hold his phone, while Alona had one on her neck.

Once around back, they opened the sliding door quietly and stepped in. Karakras took a moment to sense his surroundings. He heard no sound and sensed no movement. There was a light smell in the air of cooked food, and a bit of a heavy chemical pine smell. That smell concerned him somewhat, as it did not seem natural. He nodded toward Alona, and they started down the hallway to where Cai had told them the dining room was.

As they approached the dining room, the soft, gloomy glow of the candles indicated to Karakras and Alona that people had been there recently. They peeked inside and saw a table set for the holidays, but no one was sitting around it. It didn't look like any food was served. Some people had sat down for dinner, but it never happened. This gave both of Sage's parents a very uneasy feeling. Where were Sage and the Dedorius family if not having dinner?

Karakras and Alona didn't need to communicate verbally; they could naturally infer each other's feelings and intentions. They knew they had to search the house quickly to find their daughter, so they began on the current floor. They went from the dining room into the kitchen, and everything looked as it should. A holiday dinner had just been prepared, and the family was preparing to eat. They then went to the family room, and it looked like the kids had been watching TV recently. The cushions were dented from people sitting in them, and half-consumed drinks and snacks were lying about.

Karakras and Alona covered most of the main floor, and they needed to decide where to go next. There were several options open to them. There were the main stairs and a back spiral staircase near the living room. As they approached the back stairs, Alona noticed a small, dark hallway next to them, leading to an unexplored area of the main floor. They headed that way and went down an unkempt hallway, very dark and quite dusty, unlike the rest of the immaculate house they had been exploring.

As they approached the end of the hallway, Karakras felt his foot rub against something and saw that he was standing next to an area rug that was a bit askew. He pushed the carpet with his foot and saw that underneath there was a trap door. The hairs on his neck and arms stood up, and he looked at Alona, trying not to show the terror he was experiencing. Alona didn't want to look at her husband, so she bent down to grab the handle and pulled up the trapdoor slowly. A stale stench of something rotten rose from below, making them both wince. They saw a ladder that led down to an infinite blackness thick with decay, and Karakras and Alona descended into the waiting dark.

Chapter 59

Sage lay there, thinking about her situation, while the doctor prepared his equipment for the procedure. He wasn't telling her precisely what he planned to do, but Sage had a feeling it was not an operation being done in her best interests. Like, this guy wasn't going to remove her inflamed appendix or anything.

It was clear to Sage that the doctor wasn't quite right in the head. He was delusional. How could she not have seen it before? His outer mask always seemed so kind, so compassionate. But it was a mask, wasn't it, thought Sage. When she broke his illusion, she saw who the 'other' real person was and didn't like it. Who was this other man?

Sage could not move at all, so she decided to try to ask some questions to get more information. She didn't want to risk seeing that other person again, but she had to do something. Compliments and inquisitive questions were the way to get information from an emotionally-regressed egotist like the doctor; that was something Sage's mom had taught her. Looking around the makeshift operating room, Sage could see the doctor had spent the time hanging all his medical degrees and licenses on the concrete walls. That was no small task.

"All of your training and experience is impressive, doctor," Sage displayed socially appropriate deference to his expertise as she motioned to his certificates, "and is that a Harvard degree I am seeing? Wow, I had no idea you had such a high pedigree."

The doctor immediately perked up, and a big smile appeared. "Thank you, Sage! Most people don't know how much work and dedication a professional like me puts into their career." The doctor was positively beaming, "It's all about the patients for me, making them better and healing families. That is what I do, Sage. I help to rebuild families."

Sage had heard the term 'god complex' before when it came to doctors in general, and she was starting to understand more now what that term meant. This guy thought he was some sort of…savior. He believed he was so unique, talented, and brilliant that only he could heal the myriad fractures of American society.

"I can see that, doctor," Sage nodded toward his family of corpses sitting around the operating table. "You have done quite a job keeping your family together after such a traumatic event." Sage knew this may be poking the bear, but she had to keep this guy talking. She needed him to do something other than operate on her.

The reference to the traumatic event clicked something in the doctor's head. He stopped what he was doing momentarily and looked at her intensely, "Sage, I love my family so much, I would do ANYTHING for them. When we got into that car accident, I thought I had lost them all. That was unacceptable to me. With all my skills and talents, I knew I could save them, and I did! I healed my family and brought them home so I could care for them myself." Sage could see a tear building up in the doctor's eye.

Sage looked closer at the 'family' the doctor was referring to. She didn't want to before, but thought she should. Aside from being dressed in their Christmas outfits, Sage could see they were all wearing wigs. She guessed it made them look more life-like to him. Instead, they just looked creepier. She also noticed the wife was wearing her glasses, and one of the kids had a watch on. An illusion was being created here, and it was all for the doctor's benefit.

Sage's senses were getting sharper now. She noticed that the corpses had something else attached to their dried-out skin. What she saw wasn't all over the crepe parchment paper-like skin, but was only on the joints and connecting parts of the bodies. All at once, Sage's brain made the connection. She was seeing large black cloth stitches holding the different body parts together. She could see stitches on the wife's neck and the kid's arms and legs.

Sage then noticed something that made her blood run cold. The doctor's daughter, Macy, was missing the middle finger on one hand.

Chapter 60

Karakras and Alona went down the ladder into the depths. It seemed to Karakras that this ladder was too long for a standard basement ladder. He grimly thought this level had been extended and lowered as a special project. Karakras put each foot down slowly, looking for the bottom of the ladder, but it wasn't coming. They just kept going down, lower and lower. Then, all of a sudden, Karakras heard a crack and felt his foot fall through the now broken rung he was leaning on. He lost his grip and fell off the ladder, slamming down to the dirt ground at least ten feet below, landing on his heel. The pain radiating through Karakras' body was immense.

Alona was in shock, "Karakras, are you OK?" she whispered below.

It took Karakras a moment to regain his composure. He needed to make sure his wife got down safely first. "It's all right, honey; one of the rungs on the ladder broke," or it was cut, he thought to himself. "Come down slowly, and watch out for that." He shone his phone light at the ladder so she could see what to avoid. She quickly made it down and checked Karakras' injuries. It looked like he may have broken his ankle.

"You need to lean on me, my love. I will shoulder your burden," Alona said, helping Karakras get back on his feet and giving him someone to lean against. Karakras knew he could always count on his wife; they were forever intertwined as partners in their journey through life.

"We need to move more carefully, Alona. It is possible that the ladder was cut on purpose." Alona did not respond; she understood the gravity of his statement.

After standing up in the low light, Alona saw a switch on the wall. She clicked it, illuminating a series of industrial-looking overhead light bulbs that looked like they came from a psychiatric hospital in the 1960s. It was not a comforting glow, she thought, that was for sure.

They also noticed a contraption at the bottom of the ladder that looked like an elevator or a dumb waiter. There were buttons for up and down, and they seemed to be standing on a metal plate that could be raised or lowered. Karakras thought it was probably used to move heavy things in and out of the lower area. Anything that couldn't go up and down a ladder, like medical equipment or a body, Karakras thought.

They slowly advanced down the hallway. The lights were flickering, and a few of the bulbs were out. The feel down here was nothing like the rest of the home. It was dusty, dingy, dark, dank, and depressing. It was medical and industrial in some way, but in a sick way. Dying and decrepit was the atmosphere here. Cobwebs on the walls showed that no one had cleaned in here for some time, perhaps for years.

After a short time, they came to a large metal door at the end of the hallway. Again, this door looked like it belonged in some old mental asylum for the criminally insane. The door was made of greenish oxidized metal, rusting in patches, with large bolts and plates covering its face. There was a large metal handle, but neither Karakras nor Alona could see any keyhole. It might have been bolted from the inside, and if so, they had no idea how they would get in.

Well, there was only one way to find out. Karakras stopped leaning on Alona, reached out with both hands to grab the handle, and was met with such an electric shock that he involuntarily jumped out of his sandals by about three inches and fell to the ground, unconscious, twitching as he did.

Chapter 61

Sage was starting to panic. The drugs had worn off her by now, and some serious fear was setting in. She was strapped to an operating table by a delusional doctor who believed his long-dead family was currently alive and well. This doctor also had delusions of grandeur and thought himself the source of all that is good and decent in the world. He was so confident in his righteousness and mission that anything he did to support that goal was deemed acceptable. Even worse, this guy wanted Sage to be a permanent part of his family, and she was beginning to understand what that meant. This was a dangerous man, thought Sage. So innocent-looking on the surface, so twisted and deranged deep within.

Her brain was making connections, going back days, weeks, now months. The finger they found, the one they had been searching for since the beginning, the one that cute cat had brought them way back when. Could it be? Could that be Macy Dedorius's finger? Was the child they were looking for all along dead for ten years? It would make sense, given how hard it was for them to track her down. And how was this connected to the high-end ID operation being run out of the Inner Mind Tattoo and CBD shop and hospital morgue? Perhaps there was something there.

"Do you do all of this alone, doctor?" Sage acted innocent and questioning as if she were having a casual conversation during a checkup. "It seems like a lot of work for just a single person, even someone with your experience and qualifications."

The doctor was engrossed in his work and preparing for the operation, so he didn't think much before responding, "Oh, Sage, from time to time, we all need a little help. Keeping three people healthy all these years takes effort and collaboration. I couldn't be more appreciative of everyone who has made this possible."

Sage took that as confirmation that he had help. This guy had to get body parts, and where would be a better place than the Old Springs Community Hospital Morgue? But now he had gotten his own body, her body, and she knew which part of her he wanted first: her middle finger.

Chapter 62

Alona was trying to wake Karakras up after his shock. He was out for about thirty seconds when he finally started to come to. Alona was relieved; she had no idea what damage that amount of electricity might have done to her husband.

"Karakras, can you hear me?" Alona waved her hands and snapped her fingers in his ears, trying to get him fully cognizant. "My love, are you alright?"

Karakras did not know what had happened. He tried to remember. They were coming down this old hallway, and he touched a door handle. He now remembered the pain and how everything went black. He realized he had been electrocuted. He could feel his hands tingling, and his arms were shaking like he had been using a gas-powered weed trimmer all day. Karakras knew what that feeling was like, as it was the only job most of his people were permitted to have.

"I think so." He wasn't sure; Karakras had never had that level of shock before. "The door must have been rigged, just like that ladder. Alona, we need to be much more careful. All is lost if we get hurt before we get to Sage." The time for mincing words was over; he needed his wife to understand the danger.

"I understand," she replied, fully realizing the scope and severity of the danger they and their daughter were in. "But Karakras, how do we get in there?"

Karakras took a moment to reflect. He went into a self-hypnosis meditation for a moment, something he had learned to do long ago, and the answer came to him almost instantly. "There was most likely a single charge attached to the door. My shock should have dissipated it, and it should be harmless until it gets manually recharged."

Alona looked at him. "Are you serious? One of us needs to try it again."

Karakras nodded in the affirmative. He tried to get up to try the door again when Alona pushed him back down.

"No, my love, you cannot try it again. It may kill you if you are wrong. I will try the door."

Karakras wanted to push back on her, but he knew the truth she spoke. He acquiesced and watched his wife put her hands on the door handle. As she grabbed it lightly, there was no shock, and the door easily came open with a light pull.

Chapter 63

Sage was really freaking out now. She was breathing heavily, wrestling with her restraints, and looking for any way out of her current situation. She was utterly helpless. Things were getting real by the minute. No, by the second. Who was going to save her? She told her parents where she was, which was good. But they didn't know she was in any trouble. And Hudson and Cai must still be outside waiting for her to finish dinner. Dinner, for God's sake! Some dinner. She was the main course, apparently. To be used as replacement parts for this maniac's family of mummified corpses! She kept looking down at her finger, wondering what it would feel like if he cut it off. She decided to ask, hoping to slow him down.

"I appreciate how open and informative you are, doctor, about your expertise. Who knows, maybe someday I will follow in your footsteps." Sage knew she had to stroke his massive ego to keep his interest. "For instance, the procedure today. Will you be using any anesthetic?" Sage thought that was a good starting question.

The doctor immediately stopped what he was doing. He was intrigued by his newest daughter's inquiry. What a fine addition she is going to make! So clever.

"Why yes, of course, sweetie," he came closer and patted Sage on the head. "I will use both a local anesthetic on your hand and a general one that will allow you to stay conscious but unable to remember the event afterward. It is a minor procedure, but it will allow you to be part of our family forever!" The doctor had a maniacal look on his face for a split second.

He quickly calmed, looking at Sage with a fatherly expression, "Sage, I want you to know I would never hurt you. You are part of my family, and I will love and protect you as I do everyone else. You will be treated no differently." The doctor's expression then became sterner. "But as the father, I am the provider and protector, and I sometimes have to make difficult decisions about what's in the family's best interest. Sometimes, one family member needs to sacrifice something for another. Now, Macy needs your help, and I know you wouldn't mind making a small sacrifice for your sister."

As the doctor was talking, he was motioning to the mummified girl. Sage thought, keep telling yourself what you want, doctor, but this dead girl doesn't want anything from me. It's all about your needs, your wants, and your fantasy. Sage realized men like the doctor liked to offload their accountability onto others, consistently positioning themselves as supporting others in some self-sacrificing capacity. The doctor was always right. The doctor had all the answers. And he would solve all the world's problems as he saw them. Whether other people liked it or not.

Chapter 64

Karakras was up on his feet and was leaning even more heavily on Alona, who had now taken the lead. He was disoriented but was recovering quickly. It seemed like the electric shock was intended to maim someone, not kill them. Karakras wasn't sure if he was lucky or not. It didn't feel that way.

Alona edged into the dark room. She felt along the inside edges of the metal door for a switch and found one. With a click, the overhead lights came on and were clearly in some storage area. To the left and right were large metal canisters with warning labels. Alona could see words like oxygen and nitrogen and warnings like flammable. It looked very much like a storage area for a small medical or industrial facility.

In addition to the metal canisters, dozens of boxes towered over them, obscuring their view of the room, which was longer lengthwise than wide. Wary of traps, they inched forward, looking around them for more surprises. As a result, it took both of them a few seconds to realize that within ten feet, the rows of boxes had been replaced by a different kind of item. Karakras and Alona gasped lightly in unison as their minds comprehended what was before them.

It was like something out of a horror sci-fi movie. 'Alien' was the first one that came to Alona's mind. There was a series of glass canisters, from small to large, all on pedestals or other platforms, each filled with a greenish fluid. Even worse was what floated in the liquid. There were body parts—all sorts of body parts, in all shapes and sizes. Alona felt ill. This was not healthy medical behavior. Something sinister was at play here. Karakras knew that all he saw were his visions coming to the forefront and manifesting in reality. He knew somewhat what kind of monstrosity he was going to find here. But knowing and seeing it are two different things.

The smell was overwhelming. It was a mix of chemicals and the putrid stench of decaying flesh. Alona wondered why they smelled like dead flesh when the body parts in the glass canisters seemed well-preserved. Then she noticed some coolers on the floor and knew, without looking, that they must be filled with other, less desirable body parts. What was this monster doing, Alona wondered? What need does a reputable doctor have for a bunch of well-preserved human body parts? Nothing decent that she could think of. Maybe he was selling them, as she had heard of people going to Mexico and losing a kidney and waking up in a tub with ice. No, that wouldn't make sense. If you were harvesting organs in the jars, there would be hearts, kidneys, and whatever made money on the open black market. The ONLY thing in these jars was body parts, like arms, legs, hands, and feet. There were no internal organs. Weird.

Past all of that, in the corner, Alona saw a small table, like a makeup table. A mirror and some small jars containing ointments and lotions were on it. Around the table, there were a series of wigs on stands. These included a few smaller wigs that looked child-sized and another longer wig that looked appropriate for a grown woman. Was this guy some deranged deviant, wondered Alona? What the hell was he doing to our daughter? With that disturbing thought, she finally saw what they were looking for: a door to the next room. This door wasn't quite as scary as the last one; it was just a regular door with a knob. Alona reached for the knob and grabbed it before Karakras could stop her.

Chapter 65

Sage continued to try to engage the doctor with small talk and questions about his background and family. Eventually, he stopped taking the bait and began preparing for the surgery. He was a professional, after all, and this is what he did for a living. The doctor didn't pay too much attention to what Sage was saying. The chatter of patients and nurses was just the background noise of the life of a healer. She was a sweet kid, that was for sure, the doctor thought. She had nothing to worry about; he was sure of that, too.

"Sage, I appreciate how patient you have been." The doctor was putting on his biggest smile for her. "This is going to be a very minor procedure, and when we are done, you will be a full member of our family. Won't that be wonderful!"

Sage tried to respond, but it was clear the doctor was no longer listening. He just nodded, smiled, and continued with his preparation and work. He was currently explaining to her what he was doing, like talking to an intern or student or something.

The doctor was preparing a needle. "Sage, this is a numbing injection, or a digital block anesthesia. This will ensure you have no pain in your finger." Before Sage could say anything, he stuck her with the needle in her hand, and she winced from the pain. The doctor saw that it hurt and apologized immediately.

"Now, I am just going to wash the area with a saline solution to ensure everything is clean and there are no infections. In medical lingo, we call this debridement." The doctor loved to express his knowledge to unwilling listeners; that was certain, Sage thought. She could feel her hand beginning to numb now. She was running out of things to say and of hope. What the hell was he going to do with her after he took her finger? Was she going to become a dried-out mummy like the rest of his family?

The doctor moved one of the metal canisters closer to the operating table. Attached was a plastic face mask, which he put over Sage's head and strapped to her. "Sage, this is nitrous oxide. This will make the procedure more tolerable. It's not critical, and I wouldn't do it for any patient in my practice, but you are special. You are now a full member of our family, and as such, you deserve special treatment." Sage quickly began to feel intoxicated from the nitrous oxide. She started to smile. What the hell was she smiling about, she wondered. This wasn't funny at all.

With that, the doctor moved his operating utensil tray closer to Sage. On that tray were various scalpels, cutting scissors, retractors, clamps, and forceps. The doctor looked down at Sage's hand, thought for a second which tool was right, took a medium-sized scalpel, and leaned down to relieve Sage of her burdensome middle finger.

Chapter 66

Karakras tried to stop Alona from reaching for the door handle, but he was too slow. When she grabbed it, he flinched as he waited for the shock that had sent him unconscious. When it didn't come, he was immediately relieved. If Alona had undergone the same pain he just did, he couldn't have lived with himself. What kind of husband and father doesn't protect his wife and daughter? Karakras felt deep shame but pushed it to the back of his mind. They had a priority right now: ensuring their daughter's safety. Everything else could wait.

As the door inched quietly open, a bright light entered the room. They could see overhead lights like in a surgery room or hospital. There were all sorts of machines, gas canisters, and tables full of electronics and medical equipment. It was obvious to them that this was the room they were seeking. In the middle of the room, which they could not quite see since their view was blocked, there seemed to be a table surrounded by equipment, with metal devices on rolling tables gleaming in the fluorescent lights.

A large, older man, in his white doctor's smock and baggy blue face mask, had his back to them, engrossed in his work. Alona knew right away that this was their family doctor, Dr. Dedorius. What was this madman doing, and where was her daughter? Just then, the doctor moved out of the way to get something. After he had, they got a clear view of the operating table, and their daughter, Sage, was strapped to it with leather straps. She was heavily medicated and barely conscious.

The doctor turned around with a scalpel now in his hand and bent down closer to Sage and her hand. Instinctively, Alona and Karakras screamed, "GET YOUR HANDS OFF OUR DAUGHTER!"

Doctor Dedorius heard and turned around in surprise and shock. His face went from a kindly doctor to a deranged psychopath within a second. He then threw the scalpel he was holding at them, forcing them to close the door for a few seconds. The scalpel stuck in the door as a professional knife thrower had thrown it. The doctor moved quickly to unstrap Sage from her table and bent over to pick her up. Karakras reopened the door as he did, and Alona shot a blow-dart arrow into the doctor's back. He flinched for a second, but it did not drop him. He steadied himself, picked up Sage, and began carrying her towards the opposite side of the operating room.

Karakras steadied himself and shot another arrow into the doctor's back, and this one hit him harder, and he wavered, but still, he kept going. Karakras was surprised; regardless of weight, two darts usually dropped any man or woman. He must be pumped up on adrenaline, he thought. If Karakras could walk, he would have run after the doctor and tackled him, but he couldn't. Alona was supporting him and wasn't sure what to do either. She took her phone and called 911. It was time. They took this as far as they could, she said to herself.

The doctor knew this place better than they did; he had created it. He had built a secret emergency exit when he set up this room. So, he limped there with Sage and pushed through some curtains, which revealed a storm door that led out of the basement area on the side of the house. Ironically, this side of the house had no Shuar present, as they expected someone to come out of the back or front door. He stealthily climbed the stairs and headed to the

front yard and his waiting car underneath the shining full
moon above.

235

Chapter 67

Hudson and Cai were still up in the tree, watching the livestream with everyone else. From the perspective of the live stream, they could only see the point where the doctor walked through the curtains in the back of the operating room. It was not until he came around the side of the house, with Sage in his arms, that they knew he had gotten out.

When they saw him, the two Shuar in the front yard came out of the bushes, and Hudson and Cai jumped down from the tree to confront the doctor. Alona and Karakras came from around the corner quickly behind the doctor. The doctor attempted to walk towards his car, but as the poison from the blow darts fully kicked in, he weakened and slowed his walk. His legs became rubbery until he fell to his knees, holding Sage in his arms.

Just then, the sound of sirens could be heard in the distance. Flashing lights turned the doctor's pasty white face into a surreal nightmare. Half a dozen police dressed up in body armor and armed with AR-15s jumped out of their cars and pointed their guns at everyone—the doctor, as well as the onlookers.

"GET DOWN NOW!" The police voices were shaking with fear, "OR WE WILL SHOOT!"

Jesus, thought Hudson, calm the fuck down, we already did your job for you. Everyone, including the doctor, got down on the ground fast, hoping not to be shot by the jittery police. The police went around and zip-tied everyone, putting the doctor in the back of a squad car while they talked to Alona and Karakras and got the whole story.

Sage's parents told the police that their daughter came to have dinner with their family doctor, and he kidnapped her and tried to cut her finger off. And he is nuts and has a bunch of dead bodies and body parts in his house. This guy may even be a serial killer, for all they know. When they came over to pick her up, they went in an open door to find her, but no one answered.

The cops briefly admonished them for technically breaking the law, telling them they should have called the police as soon as they had a concern. Karakras and Alona acted with inappropriate deference to the cop's authority, which seemed to satisfy them.

After that, the cops spoke briefly with the doctor. He openly admitted everything but said that he was sure Sage wanted to be part of his family and that he was not hurting anyone anyway. Her finger would have become Macy's, as sisters do for each other. He also told the police that his family could vouch for his character and that his wife could post bail for any amount required. The cop looked at him, astonished, realizing this man was not connected to reality. He honestly thought his family was alive and well, and it looked like he either bought body parts or killed people to get what he needed to keep the illusion of a living family going. The officer thought this would provide quite a career boost if played right.

After the confession, they booked the doctor for kidnapping and abusing corpses, with more charges to come soon pending further investigation. As the police car he was in was about to pull away for him to be processed, he yelled to Sage out of the car window, who was now huddling with her family in shock.

"SAGE!" The doctor looked upset and hysterical. "Please look after my family! They need someone until I can get out. They can't take care of themselves. Please help them!"

Despite everything he did, Sage felt bad for him. He was a deeply disturbed person. Yes, he was dangerous, but he wasn't living in reality. His senses were so distorted that his sense of right and wrong had become inverted. Perverted. By refusing to let go and deal with his grief from his family's death, the doctor needed to create and then maintain an illusion. A fantasy that, for him, is so real it's more real than reality. Maintaining the fantasy became his life quest at the expense of anyone and anything.

After the doctor was driven away, the remaining police went into the house to look for other victims and came out quickly. Hudson could hear the cops talking. They had to call in a full forensic team and bring in the State Police with additional resources. Within minutes, more official vehicles, including an ambulance, approached the house. Support specialists in full hazmat gear entered the home, and soon, a helicopter was heard overhead, shining spotlights below.

Chapter 68

Hudson and the Cereal Club were having their daily cereal, as was their way, and were discussing how things had progressed with the case over the past two weeks. Hudson was looking over the blogs and social media chatter, while Cai was discussing a couple of news programs she had seen about the case. Sage just hung back and listened. She was still undergoing some residual mental health struggles since her abduction, but there was no place she felt safer than with her friends. Well, ok, maybe her family, who saved her life. Sage smiled, thinking about how many people loved and cared about her. She was lucky in that area, that was for sure. A few more minutes, and she would have one less middle finger. She looked down at her finger, grateful for it still being there.

The details of the case were now making national news. This was understandable, given the shocking and bizarre series of events. The situation became clearer through interviews with the doctor, interrogations of the morgue attendant, Nico from the inner mind, and hospital records.

About ten years ago, Doctor Dedorius and his family were in a horrific car accident, which everyone already knew. What people did not know is that the whole family, other than the doctor, died in the hospital following the crash. The doctor could not accept that they had passed, as he believed that he had the power to save them no matter what. Reality and his inner mind could not coexist with each other. So, his subconscious took the steps necessary to protect his active mind from trauma, and that was to pretend that his family never died and to fake the circumstances surrounding their death.

No one is quite sure how he pulled it off, but obviously, he had made arrangements with the morgue attendant to take the bodies home after their demise. He then faked their records, which isn't too hard when you are a doctor, so they appeared to suffer from a recoverable accident. He brought them home in the dead of night through the hospital's back door and set up his house so that he could 'take care' of his homebound family. Through the doctor's connections, he was able to get all the equipment and materials he needed to maintain his deceased family and create the illusion for himself that they were still alive. After all, that is all that mattered to the doctor—to manufacture and maintain the illusion that his family was still alive to alleviate his guilt and trauma.

For the doctor to maintain the illusion that his family was still alive, he needed them to look and act like his family. So, he dressed them up every day, just like real people. He kept the home just as they had lived there. He turned on the TV so they could watch and helped his wife cook meals. He both messed up and cleaned the house as a real family would.

Initially, the house was too quiet when he brought them home; it didn't sound alive. So, he took some old recordings of the kids and his wife and put them on a loop so he could always hear their chatter throughout the day. Anyone eavesdropping would have thought a full living family was in this home, going through their daily lives.

After some time, it became apparent to the doctor that to maintain the illusion, he needed to put more effort into keeping his family's disintegrating corpses. They were rotting after only a few days, and eventually, pieces began to fall off—an ear here, a toe there. So, the doctor became a skilled taxidermist, which is someone trained in stuffing dead bodies and treating their skin and other features into an illusory state of near life. With wigs, makeup, jewelry, and clothes, the doctor's illusion was complete.

But over time, he discovered he would need replacement parts for his family. Things get bumped, nicked, and whatnot. So, the doctor went to the morgue at his hospital and colluded with the attendant to procure various body parts to be used in his familial corpse maintenance routine. This worked for some time.

Eventually, the body parts the doctor was getting through the Old Springs Community Morgue weren't cutting it. Sometimes, they just didn't fit. They were too big or too small, or the wrong color. So, the doctor determined he needed better body parts and took it upon himself to get them, however necessary. From the doctor's perspective, he was doing what was required to protect his family and keep them safe. Wouldn't any other father do the same? he told himself. Such is how the infantile and delusional mind comforts itself into committing the most horrific atrocities.

These men of action convince themselves they are forever in the right, and whatever acts they take to do what they think is right are always justified. Thousands of men and women like this run the world we live in today. Some would call them paternalists, which, if you looked it up in a dictionary, would tell you they are people in positions of power who restrict the freedom of those below them in their 'supposed' best interest. They know what is best for you and will tell you how to live and what to think. You do what you are told. Get it?

When the doctor needed replacement body parts, he went out to get them. First, he started going to cemeteries and digging up the recently deceased. But many of those bodies were already treated by ghoulish morticians, and he was having the same issue as with the bodies from the morgue. They were either the wrong size or color or didn't match. For the doctor to get the right body parts to match each family member, he needed to scope out living people who matched the family members in the recesses of his mind. People who would be good additions to his family. And as those new members helped replace missing parts of his core family unit, they, too, became part of the core unit.

You see, in the doctor's mind, his victims would live eternally as part of his family. From his perspective, it was an honor for them to be considered by him. After all, the Dedoriuses were a top family in the town and community. He made a good salary and was highly respected, and why shouldn't a young person like Sage, an Indigenous child from a low-income family, want a leg up and be part of something she could never typically experience? The doctor was really doing Sage a favor by permitting her entrance into their rarified community air.

So, when Macy lost her middle finger a few months back, the doctor threw it in the trash like all the other discarded body parts and immediately began looking for a replacement. As he had done before, he scoped out multiple targets who would be good additions to his family unit. It wasn't just about finding a tween girl; she had to have values and something to offer. He wanted someone to enhance his family and bring them some new life.

The doctor knew she was the perfect fit during his last checkup with Sage. He had a couple of other backups, but Sage was bright, empathetic, emotionally intelligent, and adorable. The doctor considered it a great honor to bestow all his family had to offer to Sage. Her future was limitless as a Dedorius. Who knows, maybe Sage would be the one child who becomes a doctor like him, someone who can carry on his work and dedication to the family unit?

It was beyond fortuitous that Sage was the one to knock on his door to bring him a Christmas present. It was providence. He knew it was destiny the second he saw her on his porch. How else would she have come to be here if they did not have a date with destiny? This was one reason the doctor thought nothing of it when he recommended that Sage tell her parents she was staying for dinner. Since this event was ordained, there would be no interruption. Sage would be a full member of his family before the night's end.

But he was wrong, which told him he had made a mistake, but only by picking the wrong person to become a family member. The doctor's impeccable moral superiority remained intact and would always be. He would forever look down on people, trying to solve the imaginary problems that only he could perceive—in his wisdom, in his piety.

Chapter 69

The doctor didn't know just how ironic it all was. Sage and her friends had found, or had delivered, Macy's missing finger from a neighborhood cat some time ago. The cat most likely got the finger right out of the Dedorius trash can. That finger began their months-long search for its owner and helped establish Hudson and his friends as child rights advocates through their online investigations. Their online presence helped elevate the doctor's story to a national level, and, aside from the news segments, there was online chatter that multiple true-crime specials would be produced on the case.

Hudson, Cai, and Sage were almost done with their cereal and their weekly check-in meeting, which was still primarily concerned with disseminating and communicating the details of The Dedorius case to their now rather sizable online followings. During this meeting, they noticed Hudson's various social media platform accounts had passed one million followers. The Cereal Club was congratulating Hudson and patting him on the back, metaphorically, when there was a knock on the door. All three kids went to the door to see who it was.

Upon opening the door, Hudson, Cai, and Sage were greeted by three adults. One of them was a middle-aged woman in a nice grey two-piece suit, and with her were two younger men who were dressed like hipsters. To Hudson, it was like they were trying to look casual and real, but they were just putting on. It was obvious to him that they were corporate posers, immediately putting him on the defensive.

"Hello, are you Hudson?" The older woman put her hand out to shake Hudson's hand. He did not acquiesce. He just looked at her hand, then back at her face, and waited for her to continue. When he did not shake her hand, the CEO of A&I Entertainment was very irritated. Who was this little brat not to shake her hand, an important and influential entertainment executive? She made sure not to show her irritation as she didn't want to do anything to sour a potential deal. She was a professional after all.

"And are you his little friends I have been reading about, Cai and Sage?" She put her hand out to them to shake, and Sage did, as was her way. Cai put her fist out and said, "I don't shake hands; I fist-bump. It's safer that way." Again, the CEO was shaken. What a bunch of snots! She didn't like these kids at all. She regained her composure.

"Ahem, are your parents home? I would love to sit down with you and them to have a discussion. I think it's something you will all be very interested in." The CEO had a big, almost too big, smile. Hudson felt the insincerity oozing off her.

"I'm sorry, but our parents are not home right now. Is there something we can help you with?" Hudson was putting on his best face, but wanted this conversation to end.

The CEO paused for a moment. She had no interest in talking to these kids; she wanted to talk to their parents. They could approve and sign things, but these kids couldn't. She figured it wouldn't hurt to prime the engine a bit—get the kids excited so they could, in turn, convince their parents.

"Well, I would like to discuss it with everyone present. But I think I can say with confidence that all of us at A&I have seen the work you did not just on the Dedorius case, but also on Where is Dylan? and The Inner Mind and Community Hospital fiasco. We think the work you are doing is amazing! You are doing a real public service here, and we wanted to help bring that out to a larger audience." The CEO waited to see the requisite look of glee and hope on each child's face.

When she didn't see it, she continued, somewhat confused, "We at A&I want to offer you the opportunity to host your own show on our network! It would be the three of you, and we would call it, now get this, The Serial Club! Because you find and hunt serial killers! What do you think?" Again, she did not see the looks of joy she usually encountered when offering poor kids a TV deal. So, she continued her sales pitch unfazed.

"Maybe I am not making myself totally clear. We are preparing to offer you a multi-year contract with A&I Entertainment for significant six-figure salaries, all to do just what you have been doing already. Solving crimes and holding criminals accountable for their horrendous behavior. I am offering you a whole new life and a future. Not just for you, but for your families."
Again, the children's faces were like stone. What the hell was going on here? Did these kids have a learning disability or something?

She decided to try to get a response again, "So, what do you think? Do you want to be rich and famous?"

Hudson looked to Cai, then to Sage. Slowly, he looked back at the CEO.

"We'll think about it."

Hudson slammed the door in her face.